REUNITED

"Danny . . . I'm sorry."

Nervous hope jolted inside him. Swallowing once, he planted a kiss on her bare shoulder. "For what?"

She shifted in his arms until she could look up into his face. "For letting things get worse and worse until there was just no turning back."

He smiled, loving her so much that he shook with happiness. "I'm sorry I didn't ask you what was wrong. It's not my way, but I want to change. I will change."

Her wet eyes searched his face for a long time, and then she sighed. "You've always been the man I want, Danny. Don't change too much." The words were a husky warble, an admission that had been difficult for her to make he was sure.

He didn't know what to say. The room hummed with the pent-up desire between them—the need, the sorrow, the desperation, the fear.

"It can be okay if we want it to be."

He waited, but she didn't offer up any denials. Blood pounded in his neck as he marveled at the sheer, promising stillness of the moment. He dipped his head closer, testing, knowing if she pulled back, he'd die inside. He closed the distance between them with achingly slow movements. She didn't pull back.

Her gaze fluttered from his eyes to his mouth just as she raked her teeth across that plump bottom lip of hers. A simple gesture, yet powerful and telling. It completely undid him. . . .

BOOK YOUR PLACE ON OUR WEBSITE AND MAKE THE READING CONNECTION!

We've created a customized website just for our very special readers, where you can get the inside scoop on everything that's going on with Zebra, Pinnacle and Kensington books.

When you come online, you'll have the exciting opportunity to:

- View covers of upcoming books
- Read sample chapters
- Learn about our future publishing schedule (listed by publication month *and author*)
- Find out when your favorite authors will be visiting a city near you
- Search for and order backlist books from our online catalog
- Check out author bios and background information
- Send e-mail to your favorite authors
- Meet the Kensington staff online
- Join us in weekly chats with authors, readers and other guests
- Get writing guidelines
- AND MUCH MORE!

**Visit our website at
http://www.pinnaclebooks.com**

ONE AND ONLY

Lynda Sandoval

PINNACLE BOOKS
KENSINGTON PUBLISHING CORP
http://www.encantoromance.com

PINNACLE BOOKS are published by

Kensington Publishing Corp.
850 Third Avenue
New York, NY 10022

All Kensington Titles, Imprints, and Distributed Lines are available at special quantity discounts for bulk purchases for sales promotions, premiums, fund-raising, and educational or institutional use. Special book excerpts or customized printings can also be created to fit specific needs. For details, write or phone the office of the Kensington special sales manager: Kensington Publishing Corp., 850 Third Avenue, New York, NY 10022, attn: Special Sales Department, Phone: 1-800-221-2647.

Pinnacle and the P logo, Encanto and the E logo Reg. U.S. Pat. & TM Off.

First Pinnacle Printing: March 2001
10 9 8 7 6 5 4 3 2 1

Printed in the United States of America

This one is for my critique group:
Terri, Maggi, Anita, and Amy.
Through sales and rejections, from first drafts to The Ends,
during streaks of inspired motivation and bouts of "I for-
got how to write!" panic, we stick together like a well plot-
ted tale.

I love you guys.

ACKNOWLEDGMENTS

Special gratitude goes out to the following people for their unique contributions to this book:

Dan (Danny <g>) and Terri Clark, for proving by example that a soul mate certainly can come disguised as a high school sweetheart. You guys made great models.

Chris Cocozza, for being the best cover artist in the entire romance industry (and I'm not biased). You totally rock, and Encanto is lucky to have you.

Dr. Leah Cooper, my knowledgeable sister-in-law, for always being there to answer strange injury questions—even late on a Friday evening after a long week of seeing patients and delivering babies (in the dead of night, mind you).

Phyllis Williams, for allowing me to use your cool nickname.

LaRita Heet, for always saying yes when I ask if you can read something.

One

From Pilar Valenzuela's journal, Saturday, September 1:

I don't know if Lilly's impending wedding is pushing me to this point, or if I'm just tired of feeling like an orphaned wife. But I can't take it anymore. He forgot our anniversary—again. Thanks to the ever-available excuse of a "work obligation," he wasn't here to wish the boys well on their first morning of school. Considering it is Teddy's first year of all-day school, well, I can't tell you how it hurt to see the disappointment in his little face when his daddy didn't show. Pobrecito.

Not to mention Danny and I still haven't made love. . . .

Man. Fourteen years of marriage I've given to that man. If you count the time we dated, we've been together more than half my life. (Scary.) I have never loved a man besides Danny Valenzuela. I always will—he's the father of my boys. But I need more than a father and provider. I need a lover and a best friend. If that makes me selfish, so be it.

I wish I could figure out when things changed and go back. Make things turn out different. But I can't, any more than I can go on living like this. A woman's gotta do

*what a woman's gotta do, no matter how terrifying. And,
I've never been more scared in my life.*

Thunder rolled, and fat, angry raindrops slapped
the windows of Pilar Valenzuela's west Denver
home. The dreary slate-colored sky gave the impression
of day's end, though it was only a few minutes
after four o'clock. She set aside her journal and released
a long sigh, her eyes fixed on the water-
blurred grayness outside. *Just perfect.* The day might
not be over, but a long chapter in her life was. The
weather seemed to reinforce how inevitable this
awful step was.

One hot tear slid down her cheek, and she wicked
it away, determined to discourage any of its followers.
She rarely cried. No sense blubbering now.
Standing, she crossed to the big brass bed and resumed
her awful task, folding the last of her husband
Danny's shirts and placing it into the suitcase.

To love and *cherish*, their vows had said. If this was
being cherished, she'd hate to experience being
taken for granted. This was the last damn time
Danny Valenzuela would bring storms to her life or
pain to her heart, so help her—

"Mama?" Pep blinked at her from the doorway, his
perplexed gaze ping-ponging from the open suitcase
to her face. Propped against the doorjamb, Pep
stood on one tennis-shoe-clad foot, the second shoe
resting atop the first. Flour dusted the Denver Broncos
T-shirt that was almost too small for him, and his
innocent eight-year-old face was smeared with the

chocolate he'd been using to make cookies with his little brother. "Are you leavin'?"

Pain shot through her. She wobbled toward him and knelt, pulling him against her until she could feel his heartbeat on her face. She may have told herself she was trying to comfort Pep with the gesture, but the opposite was closer to the truth. His warm, little-man body made her feel like, somehow, she would find the strength to get through this horrible task of ending her marriage.

"No, *mi hijo.* I'm not going anywhere. Daddy—" her words caught and her heart pounded a slow, funereal rhythm in her chest. How could she explain a failed marriage to the boys when she'd hardly grasped it herself? Would they understand without hating her, blaming her?

"Daddy has to . . . go on a trip," she finished, clearing her throat. A trip to Get-a-Clue Land, where absentee fathers and husbands realized they couldn't continually put their families last, or they'd find themselves alone.

Knowing that everyone assumed she had the perfect life hurt almost as much as admitting to herself that her so-called fairy-tale romance with her high school sweetheart was finished. Hell, Danny had barely touched her for . . . she didn't even know how long.

Sigh. Okay, she did. Six months, one week, three days, and—she checked her watch—four hours. She knew because she'd written it down, along with every other important detail in her life. Keeping journals as she had since she was a young girl was a double-edged sword. Yes, she had a chronology of the good times, the memories and milestones. But lately, every time she reread the past few years' worth, she also faced the black-and-white reminder of all that her fraud of a marriage lacked.

Danny missed dinner tonight and didn't call. I was worried.

Danny forgot Pep's birthday party today. Pep cried.

Danny forgot our anniversary. Again. I don't care anymore.

She fought the urge to scream. Perfect life? Ha! As long as she could remember, she'd been the one to accommodate, to compromise, to make things better. *Smile and the world smiles with you.* Damn, she was sick to death of it.

Now, if not making love for six months was the only rock on her marriage path, she could work around that. She certainly wasn't so shallow that she'd give up a fourteen-year marriage over six sexless months. But things had started changing when Pep was born, and he was eight now. The lack of physical intimacy was just a symptom of a much larger underlying rift. It wasn't that Danny treated her badly or abused her in any way. He had simply forgotten she existed, which she couldn't live with. Whoever said apathy was worse than hate was a damned smart cookie.

"When's daddy comin' back?"

Pep's plaintive question yanked her back to reality. She blinked several times, unsure how to answer. "I don't know, baby." She smiled tenderly at him. "Where's Teddy?"

"Downstairs watchin' *Arthur,*" Pep said, referring

to his six-year-old brother. "We're ready for the oven. We did all the dough balls on the cookie sheet."

"Good boy." She ruffled his soft crew cut, a style both he and Teddy wore and loved. "Any problems?"

"Nuh-uh." He scratched his chin, where some melted chocolate was beginning to dry. "Teddy dropped a few chunks on the floor, but he picked 'em up and ate 'em, so the floor is still clean."

Pilar cringed at the mental image of how her kitchen probably looked right now. That and the fact that her son had been scarfing raw cookie dough straight off the floor. But what the heck? She'd mopped the day before. The boys couldn't do permanent harm spooning cookie dough onto a sheet—or eating it off the floor, for that matter. Besides, she had desperately needed the time alone to think.

And pack.

She took Pep's hand in her own and stood up. "Come on. After the cookies are done and you yard monkeys take baths, I'm taking you to spend the night with Auntie Esme and Uncle Gavino." Esme Jaramillo-Mendez wasn't a blood relative, but she, Pilar, and the third musketeer in their little band of pals, Lilly Lujan, had been best friends since high school. As far as Pep and Teddy were concerned, Lilly and Esme—and now the men in their lives, Enrique and Gavino—were family. Pilar agreed. "How's that sound?"

"Cool!" Pep brightened. He loved his "Unca'vino," due in part to Gavino's big, rumbly black truck. Her sons were hard-core vehicle freaks. *Just like their daddy.*

As though a fresh and amazing idea had popped

into his head, Pep sucked in an excited breath. "Can I—?"

"Yes, beetle bug." She chuckled. "I'm sure if you ask politely you can sit in Uncle Gavino's truck."

Pep's face lifted into a mask of amazement. "How'd you know I was gonna ask that?"

"I'm your mama." She bent and kissed him on the head, then smacked him lightly on the rump. "I know everything."

They started down the stairs. "But . . . you don't know when Daddy's comin' home, do you?" Pep's little voice sounded searingly grave and much too wise to the reality of the modern family. Make that *broken* family. Man, he was only eight years old. *This is going to be sheer hell.*

"Hello!" Pilar called out, before pushing open the unlocked front door and entering Esme and Gavino's house in Washington Park. She stomped the rain off her shoes onto the mat and looked around the lamp-lit hallway. The house seemed so warm and welcoming, as opposed to her home, which lately had seemed about as inviting as a body bag. Pep and Teddy, toting sacks of oven-warm cookies, took off at a run to find their favorite truck-owning uncle.

"Don't run, boys! Your shoes are wet." They continued unheeded, and Pilar didn't have the energy to scold.

"We're in here," called Esme from the vicinity of the kitchen. Muffled laughter danced through the house, waltzing with the aroma of fresh coffee. Lilly and her soon-to-be-husband, Enrique, were also there. Happy couples wiling away a bad weather Saturday together, probably discussing Lilly and Enrique's impending wedding—something Pilar didn't think she could stomach at this point.

Maybe I should've called first.

Pilar sighed, feeling so out of the loop. For the longest time, she had been the only one living in happy coupledom. Now Esme and Gavino were married and expecting their first baby in November. Lilly and Enrique were so much in love, it hurt to look at them. She was the consummate fifth wheel. The divorcée. Soon, anyway.

She set the boys' overnight bags aside, then shrugged listlessly out of her raincoat and shook it over the mat before hanging it on the bentwood hall tree. For the first time in her life, she didn't look forward to seeing her two best friends. She dreaded their shock when they learned she was leaving Danny. *Leaving Danny.* The thought was still so surreal.

"There you are."

Pilar spun around, her hand on her chest. Beautiful Lilly, who had recently retired from her long, successful modeling career, peered around the corner of the living room, luminous green eyes smiling down at her. Considering the foot of height difference between five-eleven Lilly and herself, Lilly always smiled *down* at her.

"You scared me," Pilar breathed, her voice too airy, too brittle. She was teetering on the brink.

Lilly tilted her head in curiosity. "What's taking you so long, girl? You forget the way to Esme's kitchen?"

"No. I just . . . I was . . ." Pilar's nose burned, her throat ached, her muscles felt heavy and inept. She'd managed to stave off every potential crying bout since she'd made peace with her decision, but right now, she had the overwhelming urge to fling herself facedown on the floor and bawl like a baby. But she was a grown woman and a mother.

Soon to be a single mother.

Don't cry. Don't cry. Don't cry. Unable to stop the pain, Pilar slumped onto the bottom step of the staircase and surrendered to the tears.

"Pea, what on earth is wrong?" Lilly squatted in front of her. "Did you have a car accident?"

Pilar shook her head.

"PMS?"

"No. I'm sorry. I shouldn't c-cry." She felt her friend's arms encircle her. Resting her face on Lilly's shoulder, she reached up and smeared at the tears blurring her vision in time to see Esme waddling into the hall.

Esme stopped short and nudged up her fashionable new eyeglass frames. "What happened?" Fear laced her voice.

"I can't believe it has c-c-come to this," Pilar slurred.

"Mama?" came Teddy's tiny, frightened voice. All three women glanced toward where he stood tentatively in the archway to the living room. "What happened to my mama?" Tears cracked his words, his eyes round and serious. His little chest heaved with frightened breaths.

"Oh, *hijito,* it's okay," Lilly soothed, beckoning him over. "Your mom just—"

"Stubbed her toe," Esme blurted, "and she's being a big baby. That's all."

Teddy glanced from Lilly to his mother, questions in his troubled eyes. "Mama? You have an owie?"

She struggled to give him a reassuring smile. "I'm okay, baby. It doesn't hurt much." *God, how it hurt.*

"Want me to kiss it?" he asked in a solemn tone.

Pilar sniffed loudly and held out her arms for her big, brave boy. She didn't know what she'd do without these kids. "Come here, you. Kiss me, instead."

Teddy scampered into his mother's arms and she showered his face with tear-moistened kisses. He settled onto her lap, nestling his head in the crook of her neck. She could smell his wind-whipped little boy scent and the chocolate chip cookies on his breath. It didn't surprise her they'd dug in already, and really, what did it matter? The cookies would spoil their dinner, but no more than finding out their mama and daddy weren't going to live together anymore.

"See?" Lilly tucked a lock of long black hair behind her ear and flashed him a Colgate smile. "Mama's all better."

"Mama looked like she was gonna cry earlier when she was packin' daddy's clothes up, too," said Pep, who had just come into the hallway. His tone was matter-of-fact, too wise.

"Pep," Pilar chastised, softly.

Blotches of red stung his cheeks, and he darted glances at the adults before hanging his head. "Well, you did."

Pilar cast a furtive peek at her friends before lowering her gaze to the floor as well. Leave it to Pep to bust her in front of her friends.

After a moment, Esme leaned into the living room, bracing her lower back with a fist. "Gavino?" she called. She turned a falsely bright face to the boys. "You guys want to go outside with your uncles and look at the truck?"

"Nah. We'll stay here with my mom," Pep said.

"Yeah," Teddy chimed, snuggling closer to his mother.

Gavino's muscular form darkened the archway, and one glimpse of the smoldering, love-wrought look he exchanged with Esme caused Pilar's tears to come anew. She remembered the heated glances Danny had given her when she was pregnant, brimming with his own machismo at the thought of the child he'd put inside her.

Those were the good days, the memories that made the stark reality of today so unbearable. Now, when Danny spared a glance in her direction at all, he seemed to look right through her. He wasn't attracted to her anymore—that much was obvious. Granted, she did weigh twenty pounds more than she had when they married, but she'd also given birth to his two sons. Didn't that earn her the leeway of a few extra curves? Maybe she repulsed him. Maybe he'd be thrilled that she wanted out. She sniffled against Teddy's soft hair.

"*¿Qué pasó?*" Gavino asked Esme, his worried gaze on Pilar. He reached back and pulled his sleek black mane into a ponytail, securing it with a band.

"Ah, Pilar stubbed her, uh, toe." She told him so

much more with her eyes. "Can you take the boys outside while Lilly and I tend to her?" Lilly, meanwhile, spoke in a whisper to Enrique, who nodded with understanding.

Gavino grabbed Pep around the neck. "Did one of you guys kick your mother in the toe?"

Pep laughed and squirmed. "No, Unca'vino. Stop."

Gavino scooped up the younger boy. "Come on, Teddy, my man. Let's go outside."

"It's rainin'," Teddy reminded them, in a tone that clearly said he thought the grown-ups were all a little dense.

Gavino looked stumped.

Enrique stepped forward. "I need some things from the auto parts store. Perhaps you boys would like to come along?"

Gavino set Teddy down. "Great idea. And I happen to know an auto parts store that's next to an ice cream parlor."

That got the boys excited, bouncing and clapping their hands at the prospect of yet more sugar.

"Not too much," Pilar said, her voice dispirited and wan. "They just had cookies."

"We all did, and they were great," Gavino said, patting his flat abdomen. "But mama's the boss. Just two scoops instead of three, guys."

"Gavino," Esme scolded playfully.

He gave her a quick air kiss, then winked.

Teddy took Enrique's large hand and grinned way up at him. Pep followed suit, entwining his fingers with "Unca'vino's." In a wave of excited masculine chatter and a cacophony of footfalls, they headed toward the back of the house where Gavino always parked.

Pilar stared unseeing at the gleaming hardwood floor until she heard the back door slam. The house fell silent. She released a long breath and wished she could fall asleep here. Wake up later and find out it had all been a bad dream.

"Talk, Pea," Lilly said gently.

She hated that she'd broken down, and didn't even know how to start. "I'm fat," she mumbled. "I'm fat and ugly."

"Hey," Lilly added, settling cross-legged on the floor in front of her. "Stop that. You are neither fat nor ugly."

Esme indicated the distended middle of her normally pixie-thin figure. "Now, *this* is what you'd call fat."

"You're pregnant, Es. It doesn't count. But the point is, I'm through." Pilar gulped back her misery. She tucked her naturally curly hair behind her ears and felt the wet ends drip against her upper back. "I packed Danny's stuff today." The grandfather clock began to chime, but to Pilar it sounded like funeral drums. She squeezed her eyes closed.

"So Pep said. And?" Esme prompted.

"And I'm asking him to leave. For good." Esme and Lilly remained hold-your-breath silent so long, she finally opened her eyes and searched their faces for some reaction.

"Oh, Pilar," Esme whispered, the expression in her intelligent brown eyes sincerely distraught. She rested her hand on Pilar's shoulder. "That's such a big step. Maybe you just need some time apart to work things out."

"No. I'm tired of trying to keep things together. I'm killing myself to make life perfect for everyone but *me,* and it isn't even working." A short laugh devoid of humor escaped Pilar's lips. "Trust me, it's over."

"God, Pea. I don't know what to say," Esme whispered.

"Me neither," Lilly added.

Pilar tossed her head with indignance. Her now dry eyes stung. "What the hell? Danny left me long ago. He just forgot to take his physical presence with him."

"Have you guys talked about it?"

She shook her head. "Not really. We stopped talking a long time ago, too."

"Honey," Lilly said. "I'm so sorry. But I do understand. We knew you'd been unhappy."

Pilar blinked with surprise. "I thought I'd been hiding it well."

"We know you better than that," Lilly said.

"When will you tell him?" asked Esme, absentmindedly stroking the mound of her baby-swollen belly.

"When he gets home from work tonight." She gestured to the matching duffel bags slumped against the hall closet door. "I brought overnight bags for the boys, if that's okay. I don't want them to hear—"

"Of course."

A pause ensued. Pilar leaned her head against the newel post on the stairway. "You know what yesterday was?"

Esme's eyes widened and she furrowed her fingers

into the new cropped hairstyle that perfectly complimented her gamine features. "No."

"Damn him," Lilly muttered, anger brightening her cheeks.

Pilar nodded. "Yep. August thirty-first. My fourteenth anniversary. And it passed just like any other unimportant day. But never, ever again."

Dan Valenzuela heaved his black canvas work bag into the trunk of his prized Chevelle and waved good-bye to a couple shift mates in the fenced parking lot of the Denver Police, District Four substation on Clay Street. The rain-dampened cement lent a chalky, raw smell to the air and washed his skin in goose bumps. He reached for a wadded jean jacket and shrugged into it, his motions slowed by exhaustion. Swing shift had been slammed with calls right out of the chute and straight until end of watch. Bar fights, domestics, traffic altercations—why couldn't people get along these days?

He shut the trunk, then lowered himself into the driver's seat of the restored 1970 convertible. *Off duty, at last.* He closed his eyes. God, he was tired. All this overtime might be padding their savings and making him look good for the upcoming sergeants' promotion, but it was killing him. He just wanted to go home and veg out. Good luck.

An elusive but distracting presence in the form of unspoken tension seemed to have invaded their home life like an occupying force. Pilar had withdrawn into a dangerous kind of quiet in the past . . . gosh, had it been a year already? More? They never fought, but it was as if she boiled just below the surface. Never having had a good role model as far as male-female relations were concerned, Dan figured he'd best just shut up until it blew over.

He moved uncomfortably through the motions of living, always feeling like he'd made some grave misstep where his wife was concerned. Small talk didn't work, because she didn't go for it. Neither did sex, if he even remembered correctly. He didn't dare ask when her *go away* vibes were so strong. Instead, he threw himself into his work, hoping the extra money would melt the ice she'd seemed to form around her heart where he was concerned.

The thought of facing that radiating tension made him hesitate to turn his key in the ignition. Why wasn't she the affectionate, easygoing Pilar he used to know? Instead, she remained polite in a tight-lipped, conspicuously silent kind of way that made his heart pound with trepidation. What had changed?

He should ask. He knew that. But right now he just didn't have the energy, and he wasn't sure he wanted to hear the answer. He remembered feeling like this around his mother, so afraid of hearing verbal confirmation that Mom was unhappy, he'd walk on eggshells whenever he sensed something was wrong. Staying out of sight and hoping to God things would get back to normal was how he coped. It had always worked. Eventually Mom would be back to her old self, and he'd breathe a sigh of relief.

Waiting it out wasn't working as well with Pilar, however.

It had to be him, something he'd done. Try as he might, he couldn't figure out what. He worked hard and took care of them. He grabbed as much off-duty work as he could find. He hadn't told her he was up for a promotion because it was still a gamble, and the thought of dealing with her disappointment as well as his own if the cards weren't dealt in his favor was too much to bear. Plus, he rationalized, if he did get the promotion, maybe the surprise would bridge the mysterious gap that had grown between them. He was reaching for straws, but who knew, anymore?

Fatigued, he dragged his palm down his face. The bottom line was, he loved his wife and sons. He loved his career, and it gave him great pride to provide a good life for his family. But lately, something just seemed out of whack. Surely nothing serious . . .

Fellow officer, Joe Gann, rapped on Dan's window, startling him out of his thoughts. He glanced over, and Gann motioned for him to roll it down.

Dan did. "What's up, Gann?"

The tall, loose-limbed redhead jerked his thumb in the direction of an idling green Pathfinder carrying several of their other shift mates. "We're headin' to Lucero's for a few beers. You comin'?"

The damp night chill swirled into his car and mingled with the fresh scent of the vinyl polish he'd rubbed into his dashboard the previous day. Hands wrapped around the steering wheel, he considered the invitation. Beer, wings, and mindless male banter. He knew he should say no, but the stress of

Pilar's disconcerting demeanor made a no-pressure beer with the guys sound damned inviting. Really, what could it hurt?

He rapped his thumbs against the wheel—*ba-da-bum*. "You know, that sounds good," he told Joe. "I'll follow you."

Pilar woke with a start when she heard Danny's key in the lock. Her neck had stiffened while dozing in the chair, and she winced as she straightened the kinks. She glanced at the anniversary clock on the mantel—two hours late. Big surprise. So much for hashing things out. It was past one A.M., and now she just wanted him to leave.

The front door opened and bonked into the suitcases she'd left in the foyer, which she could see from where she sat. She heard the scrape of them against the tile, followed by Danny's mumbled expletive. *D-day.* She crossed the room on wobbly legs, her gaze focused on the luggage, her heart in her throat. A strip of blue moonlight reached like an ominous tentacle into the otherwise dark hallway.

She watched, filled with tingly trepidation, as Danny peered around the door. Bluish light deepened his black hair and played light and shadows on his strong jaw, regal cheekbone. Her breath caught at the exact moment he noticed the bags, and time froze.

Pilar gripped the edge of the wall.

He flicked on the hall light, and his baffled gaze sought and found her face, his eyes searching. "Pilar?"

Muscling past the suitcases into the hall, he

stopped. He clutched a grocery store bouquet of flowers—red roses, pink carnations, and white daisies. It hung limply against his muscular thigh, forgotten. *How symbolic.* Pilar couldn't take her eyes off the blossoms, and eventually Danny followed her line of scrutiny.

As though he'd just realized they were in his hand, he tentatively held them out to her. "I . . . I know I forgot our anniversary yesterday, and I'm so, so . . . I've had so much on my mind, but that's no excu—"

"It doesn't matter. Just . . . set them down."

He looked so crushed and contrite as he placed them carefully atop one of the suitcases, she almost felt guilty. She lifted her chin and fought the twinges. She'd borne all the forgotten events, the disappointments, the changes in their relationship without a single word of complaint, just like she'd been raised to do. But she couldn't placate him any longer. She had reached her breaking point.

"It does matter." He spread his arms, then let them fall to his sides. "I know it does. I'm so sorry, Punkybean."

She huffed, denying how her stomach swirled hearing his deep voice form the silly pet name he'd been calling her since she was fifteen years old. Her gaze fell to the suitcases and her mind to the emotional chasm between her and this man she'd loved for . . . so long. She couldn't look at him—at his familiar wide shoulders; brown, smooth skin; and regulation short, black hair—without knives of pain slicing through her. He was a beautiful man. Such a loss, this marriage.

"I'm sorry, too," she choked out. "Believe me." The night air billowed the hem of her ankle-length robe as his pause loomed long and thick. She forced herself to look at him, just as he glanced, again, at the baggage between them.

"Are you . . . going somewhere?" His expression was guarded.

"No." The weight of fourteen years of marriage settled on her shoulders. "You are." Her voice came out shaky, and she fought to steady it, pressing her palm against her trembling torso. This wouldn't get any easier. "The boys and I are staying here, in the house they're used to. They need the stability. You're leaving."

Danny's brows dipped and his jaw slackened. He started forward but stopped when she took a step back. "What are you talking about?" His question sounded husky, incredulous.

Having said the most difficult words, her emotions were tumbling down like the house of cards this marriage had become. She ached, but no way in hell would she cry. She wrapped her arms around her middle. "Damn you. I've loved you more than half my life, Danny Valenzuela. But I can't handle being a nobody to you any longer. I won't."

"A nobody?" Unstoppable this time, he advanced on her until she could see rain droplets glistening on his hair and skin. Back pressed against the wall, she turned her face away from his nearness and closed her eyes.

He gently pulled her chin toward him and waited

until she looked at him. "This is me, baby girl. You and me. How could you think—?"

"Stop." She smacked his hand away, her inhale pulling in the familiar pine, leather, and night-air essence of him despite her attempt *not* to smell it. "I have tried as much as I can, compromised as much as I'm willing to. This is killing me, can't you see that? It's over." She skirted past him and retreated a few steps into the dark living room, as though the shadows would cloak her in safety.

He stood utterly still, a look of horror blanching his face as he clearly tried to grasp—or deny—the meaning of her words. "What's over?"

"We are. The farce our marriage has become."

"No, Pilar. Don't say—"

"Yes, damn it! Listen to me." She clenched her hands, shoring her resolve. "I can't continue playing the role of happily ever after when everything's so wrong between us."

His chest rose and fell with harsh breaths. "So, that's it? Just like that, you blindside me? For God's sake, Pilar, if things have gone that wrong, we can make them better." He gripped her arms with desperate intensity. "It's always been you and me, Punky. How can you say it's over, like it never meant a thing?"

"I have to! Don't act like this is all of a sudden," she said, her voice shrill with emotion.

"But, it is. To me." His thumbs moved in circles on her arms. "You never even told me anything was wrong, Pea."

"I shouldn't have had to tell you." She shook off

his hold and moved around him. Gripping the edge of the door, she turned to him and set her jaw. "P-please, Danny. Just go."

He gaped like she'd lost her mind. "I won't just go. This is my *family* we're talking about. I won't give up—"

"I don't have the energy to argue," she rasped, losing her steam. "You should have been home hours ago. We could've talked then. But I'm exhausted and I'm angry. I don't want to talk to you now. Go, please. At least respect my wishes enough to give me some time and space."

He stared at her from the living room, the shadows carving deep shadows in his cheeks. His throat moved as though he was on the brink of tears. With a sharp exhale, at last, he snatched up the suitcases.

"I'll leave, Pilar, for tonight." Grim determination tightened the skin around his eyes. "But this is *not* over. We are not *over*. Not by any stretch of the imagination."

Two

Written on Dan Valenzuela's crumpled cocktail napkin from dinner, Wednesday, September 5:

> *TO DO:*
> *Wash car.*
> *Laundry.*
> *Look for apartment? (crossed out)*
> *Ask Ruben if I can stay a little longer.*
> *Talk to Pilar about the kids. About everything.*
> *Punkybean. Why?*

For the millionth time since he'd stormed out of his home a few days earlier, Danny lay wide-eyed on his brother Ruben's lumpy hide-a-bed and asked himself why he hadn't done more to change Pilar's mind that night. Why he hadn't argued more. Pleaded. Apologized until he was hoarse. Why he hadn't cried, begged. But he hadn't. Period. Instead, angered or dumbfounded by her demands, he wasn't sure which, he snatched up the suitcases she'd packed—brushing aside the wilted bouquet that was, admittedly, a pathetic gesture of apology for a missed anniversary—and left.

Ruben welcomed him to stay without asking questions, which was just what he needed. He still hadn't told his brother what was up, and Ruben knew enough about Dan's personality not to probe.

Now here he lay, unable to sleep without the familiar rhythm of Pilar's breathing beside him and knowing he didn't want to go on breathing himself if the only woman he'd ever loved was no longer in his life.

He threw his forearm over his eyes and tried to rid his mind of that awful picture of her. His itty bitty slip of a wife, her back pressed against the wall, peering up at him like a cornered doe on day one of deer season. Her dusky skin flushed with anger, disillusionment spiking the thick lashes around her huge brown eyes. He'd wanted to comb his fingers through her sleep-tossed auburn curls and kiss the trembles from her full lips. But he hadn't. Though his mind had reared up with disbelief at her words, every nonverbal cue told him she was beyond being convinced. How could he have screwed up so badly?

With a vicious exhale, he turned to his side, punched the prison pillow he'd been sentenced to use, and tried to get comfortable—a futile pursuit. The metal support bar beneath the thin mattress cut into his thigh like a dull sword, and the basement felt dank and miserable.

He glanced at the illuminated red digits of the borrowed alarm clock and scowled at the late hour. But, *his wife had left him.* Sleep was about last on his priority list.

As a boy, he'd sworn he would be a better husband and father than his dad had been. Victor

Valenzuela had callously left his wife with five young sons to support. Because of him, she'd had to work three jobs just to make ends meet. He'd valued partying more than his own family. Good-time Victor. None of it had escaped Danny's notice.

Watching his mother come home late at night, bone-weary from working, had hardened young Danny's resolve. Mama had never complained, but that hadn't mattered. When he married, Danny vowed he would show his wife how much he cared by working extra hard so she'd never have to. He'd be the kind of provider his father had never even considered being, and he'd take care of his mother, too.

And, that's what he'd done—worked so hard he barely had a spare moment. Now his mother was enjoying her retirement, and Pilar was able to be a full-time mother to Pep and Teddy, just on the money he earned. It had never mattered that he had no free time, that he often missed social events to work overtime. He had proven that sometimes the apple *does* fall far from the tree: he may share the man's blood, but he was nothing like Victor Valenzuela. He'd been proud of that until a few days ago.

Why hadn't it worked? Why had all his efforts only succeeded in driving his wife and family away? More importantly, what could he do about it? Because, no matter what it took, he wouldn't lose his wife and sons to some failure he couldn't even understand. God help him, he couldn't bear to think of it.

* * *

"This is absurd," Pilar groused at Esme as they power-walked through Washington Park the next morning. Esme had recently begun a sabbatical from the private university where she was a genetics researcher and professor so she could devote time to raising her first baby. Since Danny had left, she and Pilar had met every morning to exercise after the boys were off to school. Lilly joined them when she could, though wedding plans and work kept her very busy.

Pilar wiped her forehead with her sleeve. "*You* are seven months pregnant, yet I'm doing ninety-nine percent of the huffing and puffing."

Esme swung her lean arms in the exaggerated but controlled manner she'd learned during a recent powerwalking seminar. A quick chuckle pulled dimples into her fine-boned cheeks. "It's your short legs. Plus, I've been doing it longer." Esme gave her an encouraging smile. "You'll get used to it."

This particular morning the park teemed with walkers, runners, and in-line skaters, thanks to summer's lovely weather hanging on with the tenacity of a pit bull terrier. As she struggled to regulate her breathing and keep the sweat from her eyes, Pilar wished the days would cool off.

Pilar sighed, and mirrored Esme's arm motions, if a bit awkwardly. The weird swishy movements were hard to get used to. "Well, I hope all this sweat pays off somehow, because it sucks." She hadn't been so out of breath since . . . well, frankly, since—*damn*.

Unwelcome thoughts of making love with Danny intruded into her unprepared imagination. Her stomach clenched. In her mind's eye, however, she saw herself in her lithe high school body, not in this rounder, older, birthed-two-boys form in which Danny hadn't shown interest for months. Or had it been years? Her chest tingled. If the "no pain, no gain" credo held merit, she should be in Olympic form soon, because, God knew, she hurt—and not entirely because of the exercise.

Why, Danny? Why?

They used to be so in tune, so absorbed and in love. The first six years of their marriage had been carefree and idyllic. Passionate, too. Bigtime. Give them a flat surface and some privacy, and they were all over each other.

Then Pep had come along and things began to change, so gradually that she hardly noticed. When she compared now with then, though, the difference in their relationship was drastic. *Why* it had changed was what she couldn't quite figure. Danny had wanted the boys as much as she had, so that couldn't be it. Was it her fault? Had he fallen out of lust, then out of love with her, like so many couples these days?

"Hurry up, slowpoke. What's up?"

Pilar bit her lip, and stepped up her pace. "Sorry."

"What are you thinking about?"

The pause lasted just a touch too long, and Esme *would* catch it. Still, Pilar opted for the evasive answer. "Nothing important."

Esme stopped and turned toward Pilar, grasping her shoulders. "Pea," she said, almost roughly, "it's okay to think about him. Don't lie to me."

"I-I'm not."

Esme scoffed, but not unkindly. "Be real."

She studied her friend's worried expression before admitting defeat. "Okay, I was thinking about him."

"Naturally. He's a big part of your life, and it's only been a few days. Nothing's resolved. What do you expect?" Esme squeezed her arms, then released them. "Give yourself time."

Pilar bit her lip. "He hasn't even tried to talk me out of this."

Esme flashed her a surprised look. "You want that?"

"Well . . . no." A tight pause. "I don't know. I guess it just stings my ego that he doesn't even try."

"Pea," Esme softened her tone. "You told him to leave. Was it just a high school game? A ploy to get him to beg for your forgiveness?"

"Of course not. I . . . meant it," she finished weakly.

"And surely Danny knows you wouldn't bluff about something so serious. He's probably still reeling. You did ask him for time and space, you know."

Pilar grimaced. "You aren't making me feel better."

"I'm sorry." Esme gave her a quick hug, then studied her at arm's length. Without another word, Esme steered Pilar to a bench dappled green and gold from the sunlight reaching through the towering cottonwood above it. They sat.

"Okay, spill it. I could use a break, anyway." Esme rubbed the side of her abdomen, where the Amazing Kickboxing Baby, as he'd been dubbed, had been battering her for days. "You still love him."

No sense lying. "Yeah, but, so what? It takes more than just love."

"True. But love is a great base. It makes almost every obstacle surmountable."

"Not this one." Pilar leaned over and plucked a dandelion, twirling it absentmindedly between her thumb and forefinger. The tubular stem felt both sticky and hollow, much like her life. "I feel like a failure." Embarrassment warmed her cheeks.

"It takes two to make a marriage work and two to make it fail. Don't shoulder the whole burden."

Pilar pondered this imponderable. "Do you know . . . before he left, we hadn't made love in more than six months?" It shamed her to say it, but maybe the first step was admitting how wrong things had gone.

"Why not?" Esme looked startled. She dug through her knapsack for two bottles of water, handing one to Pilar, who set it aside.

"I don't know. The honeymoon was truly over, I guess. I could handle rejection from another man, but not from Danny." She lifted the dandelion beneath her chin and turned toward Esme. "Remember when we used to do this as kids, Es? If the yellow reflected on our skin, the boy was hot for us?"

"Pea, cut it out."

Pilar leaned forward. "It's not reflected anymore, is it? Look." Her voice cracked on the demand.

Esme sighed. "Don't do this."

"Why not?" She threw the dandelion aside, desperation welling inside her. "The boy is definitely not hot for me. I just don't know why not."

Exasperation reddened Esme's cheeks. "That's a silly kid's game, Pilar. "Whatever the problems in your physical relationship, they have nothing to do with dandelions *or* with your sex appeal." She raised a finger. "And don't bother denying that's what you're implying."

"Then what? If not that, what else could it have been?"

"I don't know. Sexual desire ebbs and flows."

Pilar huffed. "Apparently ours just ebbs."

Esme chewed the inside of one cheek. "Did you initiate?"

"I used to." *A* long *time ago,* her mind added. Pilar crossed one foot over the opposite knee and fiddled with her shoelaces. "But not lately." She had stopped offering her affection when his attention seemed to wane . . . but what came first? The chicken or the egg?

"Did you still want him that way, before——?"

"Yes. God, yes." Danny Valenzuela was well and truly the love of her life. "But I don't know if it showed. At least not at the end." Ugh. It sounded so final. "I was just . . . I don't know . . . so angry. So hurt. . . ."

"Well, what did he say when you told him that?"

"I didn't really . . . tell him, Es. But he wasn't having sex, either." She pouted. "He should have known something was wrong. He should have asked."

Esme released a humorless bark of a laugh. "Men are a lot of things, but mind readers isn't one of them. You have to communicate to make a relationship work."

"Look, it's too late. I tried to wait out this . . . rocky patch, but to be honest, things started to change back when Pep was born. I've grinned like a good little wife for way too long. I have to stand up for myself this time, Es."

Esme lifted her hands in surrender. "Hey, I support you. I just want you to be happy. But, I won't lie—I can't picture you with anyone but Dan."

"Neither can I." Nagging worry burned like swallowed poison in Pilar's stomach. In truth, she and Danny had gone from fine, to silent, to separated, without so much as one fight. Was *that* her transgression? That she'd said nothing, held everything in, until the only word she knew to say was good-bye?

"Hey, chicadees." Lilly flashed her ubiquitous cover-girl smile as she loped across the path toward them, a bundle of exuberance and joy.

"Hi, Lil," Esme said.

Pilar merely smiled. She'd never seen Lilly as content as she'd been since she'd fallen in love with Enrique and left her modeling career to start a nonprofit organization with him. Lilly might have the looks for the runway, but she had the heart for good works, and the serenity of having found her true station in life showed in her every movement. Pilar envied her that.

"I'm glad I didn't miss you guys completely." She wound her long hair into a spiky knot, securing a claw clamp over it, then said, "Scoot a cheek," to Pilar, and sat down as soon as she'd obeyed. "What kind of exercise is this, slackers? Sit and be fit?" She still hadn't seemed to notice the aura of gloom that surrounded them.

"No." Pilar leveled a bleak gaze at her. "We're trying to figure out why Danny and I hadn't made love in more than six months before the split. And, before that, why things had been getting progressively worse for—"

"Eight years, she says," Esme interjected.

Lilly's eyes darkened. "That long, Pea?"

"Yeah." Pilar shrugged one shoulder. "I couldn't seem to walk and think about that lovely topic at the same time."

Lilly patted Pilar's knee. "I'm sorry I was being so flippant."

"It's okay. You don't have to walk on eggshells around me." Impatience blasted through Pilar, directed at herself. "As a matter of fact, I'm tired of this *poor me* tune I've been whistling. Know what I need? Hot and heavy, no-strings sex. Wild, sweaty, boot-knockin' sex with a man who can make me feel like a wanton, lusty—"

"Pea!"

"—hussy."

She met Lilly's horrified gaze directly. "I'm serious. Hey—set me up with Enrique's little brother? He's gorgeous. Definitely knockable."

"You're still married!"

"Separated," Pilar corrected. "Big difference."

"*Cállate!*" Esme smacked her upper arm. "Iso was in elementary school when we graduated, for God's sake."

"So?" Pilar crossed her arms. "He's all grown up now, and a real lady's man, from what I've heard. Spending time with a hottie like Isaías Pacias would do wonders for my self-image, and—"

"I'll tell you what'll do wonders for your self-image," Lilly interrupted. "Spending some quality time with yourself. And I'm not talking about sex, so drag your mind out of the gutter and listen."

Pilar hoped her expression was appropriately skeptical.

Lilly pressed on, undaunted. "Face it, you've always put yourself last. First in high school when Danny was Mr. Football Hero and you decorated his arm. Then, college. You worked while he went to school, setting aside your own aspirations—"

"I wanted to do that, Lil."

"Granted, but you still put yourself last. And now, with the boys, you do it even more." She held up her palms. "I understand mothers have to make sacrifices, but you're a woman, too."

Lilly had hit so close to the mark, Pilar squirmed and looked away. Her faults were agonizing in the light of day.

"She's right, Pilar," Esme chimed.

"You don't need to knock boots or anything else with Iso. Perish the thought—he's practically *my* little brother." Lilly shivered. "What you need is some introspection."

"Intro*spection*?" Pilar scoffed. Sarcasm seemed as good a defense mechanism as any. "And, that's ranked above sex on Maslow's hierarchy of needs? Since when?"

"Hush, girl." Lilly squeezed her arm. "I'm saying you need to take stock of your future. You've made a major change. Now you have to figure out what to do with the rest of your life, where you want to be in five years. That's more important than scratching some sexual itch."

Pilar looked down at her hands, which were clenched in her lap. In five years? Five years! Pep would be—ugh!—a teenager. A fatherless teenage boy. She hadn't imagined it that way.

She'd thought leaving her husband was the end, but her friends were right—it was a scary beginning. All she'd ever known was being Danny's wife and the boys' mother. Just like she'd always wanted. What else was there for her?

Cold apprehension clawed up her spine. "I wouldn't even know where to start," she admitted, her voice a rough whisper.

"All the more reason for you to do it," Esme said. "You've given yourself a clean slate, but Lil's right. Now you have to fill it. You have the boys, of course, but you're only thirty-two. What else do you want to write on that slate?"

Danny.

The word popped into Pilar's mind before she could stop it. She squeezed her eyes shut, unable to imagine life without him. Yet *her* actions, her request for a separation, had made living without him a stark reality.

She wasn't happy in her marriage. Fact.

So why did the thought of ending it prompt such sparks of terror inside her? Flashes of fear? Aches of loss? *She'd* uttered the words, *she'd* set the wheels in motion. She had better damn well get used to it. And she better get used to herself—her new self.

She managed her first heartfelt, if a bit tremulous, smile of the day. "You're right. My life isn't defined by being his wife anymore. A-and, that's a good thing." She paused, drawing the corner of her lip into her mouth. "Right?"

"If you want it to be," Lilly said.

Another pang of uncertainty struck. "I just haven't gotten used to it yet. B-but, I will."

"Atta girl," Esme said, beaming. "You'll get through this if you put your mind to it. You don't need Danny."

Yes, I do.

"No," Pilar said sternly, hoping to quell the scared little voice inside her. "I don't."

Dan stood on the curb and stared, dumbfounded, at the bucked hood of his patrol car, which was wedged up against the backside of the late model Mercury Sable he'd rear-ended. He took in the glass-strewn crash scene, the bent hubcap lying in a pool of power-steering fluid—an apt metaphor for the sorry state of his life.

Truthfully, his pride stung more than the airbag cut on his chin. He'd been en route to handle a call. His mind, of course, had been filled with thoughts of Pilar, instead of focused on the job as it should have been.

When the Sable's driver braked instead of cruising through the yellow—what most drivers did when a cop was behind them, a fact he well knew—he hadn't given himself enough reaction time to stop. It was Police Driving 101, and his grade was a big, fat F. This was not an error an eleven-year veteran police officer should make.

Yet here he stood on Federal Boulevard, in the middle of the least cop-friendly neighborhood in his sector, while his supervisor, Sgt. Obermeyer, wrote the report with his name printed in the at-fault box.

He pulled the handkerchief away from his face, wincing when it tugged on the clotting blood. A glance at his supervisor showed her engrossed in the paperwork, and guilt stabbed Dan. Obermeyer hadn't shown any kind of emotion when she'd rolled on scene. Instead, she remained carefully neutral toward Dan and his mistake. Somehow that felt worse than if she'd yelled at him.

As if reading his thoughts, Nora Obermeyer glanced up from the long state accident form, the breeze catching wisps of gray-shot blond hair that had escaped from her braid. "Grab the insurance card from the cruiser for me, Dan."

Nodding once, he started toward the car, then turned back. "Sarge, I'm sorry about this." To make matters worse, they were shorthanded to start with and Fridays were always busy. Now he'd tied up not one but two cars with this mess.

"Now's not the time for apologies." She glanced toward the tow truck that had just rumbled to a stop in front of the Sable. "Get the card, then go deal with the tow driver. Report to my office after this intersection is cleared and you've swapped out cars at shops. We'll discuss it then."

Dan gave another stiff nod, then stalked toward the battered cruiser, feeling glum. Obermeyer wouldn't rip him a new one; that wasn't her style. But he could tell his long-time sergeant was disappointed, and he couldn't blame her. First his marriage, now his formerly stellar job reputation. What next?

An hour later, he rapped on the door to Sgt. Obermeyer's office, then entered, dread thick and sour in the pit of his stomach. "Am I interrupting?"

"No." Nora looked up from behind the battered metal desk, then stood. "Come in and have a seat. Actually, indulge me for a second. Come here." She walked around to the side of her desk.

Confused, Dan approached her. When he was two feet away, she leaned forward and sniffed. "Aha."

"What's going on?"

"A little intuitive experiment. My guess is, you're having wife problems and it's affecting your judgment on the job." The statement sounded confidently neutral. "That about hit the mark?"

Dan stared at her, then bent his head and sniffed. Nothing. "How'd you come to that conclusion?"

"I've been supervising men for ten years, Dan. You for three. As your supervisor and one who's trained to observe"—her eyes crinkled with wry humor— "but mostly as a woman, I happen to have noticed that Pilar uses fabric softener on your uniforms. Downy—the same brand I use."

"I don't get it."

She shrugged. "Clearly, she hasn't been the one washing your clothes, because that springtime fresh scent is history. Couple that with your uncharacteristic preoccupation of late, and it doesn't take rocket science to put it together."

No, but apparently it *did* take a woman.

The chair's dilapidated cushion wheezed as Nora settled into it, her gun belt squeaking with the motion. She adjusted her flashlight so it hung along the side of the chair, then steepled her fingers on the desktop. "In light of today's incident, it's time you and I talk about it."

Dan sank into one of the vinyl-covered swivel chairs that faced the desk, feeling dumbfounded and out of his league. For the most part, Nora Obermeyer was just another cop, and a damned good one. But every once in a while, some odd thing reminded him she was also a woman. "Fabric softener?"

"Well"—one eyebrow quirked—"do you use it?"

It hadn't crossed his mind to buy products *other* than the detergent, and truthfully, Pilar had always done the shopping and washing, at least up until last week. Pilar had done *a lot* up until last week. Chagrined, he stared at his knees. Should he have known what laundry products Pilar used? Did his lack of attention contribute to her decision to kick him out? He peered at his waiting sergeant, and his thoughts jerked back to her question. "Uh, no. I don't use it."

"My point exactly." Her hard gaze diffused into a look that bespoke of friendship more than rank. "Spill your guts, Dan. You aren't doing yourself any favors keeping it bottled up. As your friend, I care. As your supervisor, I need to determine if you can pull it together enough to work."

Dan straightened. "I can work. I just need . . . aw, hell." He scrubbed his palm over his face, then slumped back in the chair. "I need my wife back."

Nora let his words hang in the air a moment. "She left?"

"Kicked me out."

"Were you cheating on her?"

His head came up like he'd heard gunfire. "What? Never." His temperature rose at the casually posed question. How could she think . . .?

"Any physical violence?"

Dan strained forward, hot blood ripping through his temples. "Don't insult me, Sergeant."

She didn't even blink. "No need to get angry. I'm not accusing you, just trying to get the basic picture."

Teeth clenched, hands white-knuckled on the chair arms, he said, "I would never hurt Pilar or *any* woman."

Obermeyer didn't appear cowed or bothered by his vehemence. She nodded once. "Enough said. I had to ask." She flicked a hand. "Sit back."

He did. Grudgingly.

Nora crossed her arms. "Well, I'm all ears. I've been happily married to a civilian for twenty-six years and I've raised three sons, none of whom use fabric softener." She winked. "Maybe I can help."

Danny willed the anger inside him to settle. He took a moment to collect his thoughts. Then, avoiding any mention of sex, which would have been way too uncomfortable, he haltingly described the chasm of distance and silence that had grown in his marriage. He couldn't tell her how it started, or how it had gotten so bad, because he had no friggin' clue. He ended with the night Pilar had sent him packing.

When he finished, Nora's intuitive eyes were narrowed. She shifted in her chair, her weapon clanging on the metal armrest, then cleared her throat. "From what you've told me, her kicking you out doesn't make sense. You work hard, support her She stays home with the kids, which she wants right?"

"Yes."

She twisted her mouth. "Seriously, no arguments?"

He shook his head. "Pilar's never been confrontational. She never complains. She's great."

"Never complains. So, what about all the rest of the things married couples struggle with?"

"Like?"

"Money? Child-rearing? Religion? In-laws?"

Dan shook his head. "No problems. We've always seen eye-to-eye. We don't even bicker."

"Hmm." Nora drummed her fingers against her lips, searching for the elusive answer. Suddenly the drumming stopped. "Were you attentive?"

"Attentive?" Meaning what?

"Did you give her the attention she needed? You know, hugs and kisses, remembering her birthday and your anniversary. Did you bring her little gifts now and then just because you love her? That sort of thing. Attentive. It is a commonly known word, Dan."

Dan recalled the apology flowers he'd given Pilar for having missed their anniversary with a twinge of guilt. He supposed he wasn't the most attentive male on the planet, but it had never seemed to be a problem. "Well, I . . . don't have the best memory for dates." He grimaced, feeling out of step. "But Pilar knows I love her. She wouldn't leave me over something so minor as forgetting an anniversary or two."

"Granted. I'm sure it was more than just that. But women want to feel loved and special. Remember"—she raised an eyebrow—"the crime is always based on the perception of the victim. It's what Pilar thinks that matters."

He'd never thought of it that way. "But the times I missed events or forgot special days, I was working." He spread his arms wide in protest.

"So what, Dan?" Nora scoffed. "Since when does that feeble excuse work?"

Dan felt nothing but confusion. Taking care of his family was a feeble excuse? "It didn't bother Pilar, or she would've said something."

"I thought you said she never complained."

He pondered this, then dismissed it. "She knew I was working *for her,* Nora. To provide us a good life."

Nora leaned forward, her chair squeaking. "I get that. I'm sure Pilar does, too. But I bet she needed more, whether she verbalized it or not. Most women do."

Frustration squeezed his skull like the metal band on an electric chair. "Like what? She got to stay home with the kids, like she wanted. I provided for everything. She had security, freedom. Anything she needed."

"Except you." Obermeyer made a little gun with her hand and fired it at him.

He scowled, flicking away her words. "I told you. There's never been another woman besides Pilar. I love her."

"That's not what I meant. I'm talking about affection. Attention. Romance. Stick with me here."

"We . . . we had that." A sinking feeling in his stomach dragged his gaze from Nora's too perceptive face. "Then the boys came along, and I had to start thinking about their future—"

Nora's tired laugh made him feel like a child who didn't quite get it. "Damn, Valenzuela. I never knew you were so thick. How'd you win her in the first place?"

Stung by the insult, he huffed. "Thanks a lot."

"No. It was a sincere question. You won her once." She rolled her hand, urging him on. "How?"

What kind of wacko Venus question was that? "I don't know. That was in *high school*. We were kids then, not adults with a mortgage and two kids to raise, responsibilities."

The sergeant held out her hand. "But she fell in love with you for a reason. True or false?"

"True, I suppose."

"Okay." She inclined her head. "Find out why and how, and try to figure out when it ended."

He didn't get this right-brain, New Age advice. It wouldn't solve a damn thing. He couldn't be eighteen forever. For Nora to suggest otherwise wasn't practical. The issue wasn't that he'd become a different man or Pilar a different woman. The problem was, his wife had kicked him out. Period. Why couldn't women ever stick with the matter at hand?

Frustrated, he pushed to his feet and straightened his gig line, jutting his chin out to loosen the collar of his uniform shirt. "Thanks for listening, Sarge. I'll take your suggestions under advisement."

She followed his all-business lead and turned her attention to the stack of forms on her desk. "Good. Do so, Valenzuela. At *home.*"

What? Horror riddled through him. "You're suspending me for the accident?"

"Of course not, though I will have to note it in your critical incident file."

No surprises there. "Sure. But, about the time off—"

"Listen." She leveled him with a clear blue gaze that left no room for argument. "You have a lot of banked vacation time, and I strongly suggest you take it. I'm not sentencing you to hard time, for God's sake. Get your life together so your mind can focus on the job." She aimed her pointer finger at him. "You're no good to me in your current state, Dan."

Dan stood straighter. Nora was right, which rankled. "Fine," he bit out. "How long?"

She shrugged, and tapped a pile of forms into order. "It's up to you. The shift is fat, so we won't be shorthanded. But I don't want you back here until your head's screwed on straight. If that means two months, it means two months. Is that clear?"

"Crystal."

"Good. Keep me up-to-date."

An awful thought rushed into his mind, and his stomach lurched. He cleared his throat. "How will, uh, this affect my chances on the Sergeant's test? I'm on the list to take it mid-month."

Nora shook her head as though *he* were the exasperating one. "Dan. You're an officer, not a superhero. It's okay—no, it's expected—that you also have a *life,* and sometimes life gets messy. I guess it depends on how you handle it."

Another cryptic answer. "What I meant was, can I still come in and take it, even if I am on annual leave time?"

"Yes. I'll note it, and they'll expect you there."

He gave a curt nod and turned to leave.

"Hey," Obermeyer said, her tone softer.

He paused, his hand strangling the doorknob.

She tapped the end of her pen on the desk a few times as she studied him. "Think about what I told you when you're not so pissed off at me."

Heat rushed to his neck, but he held her gaze.

"That's all I ask." Though her face remained serious, a whisper of a smile showed in her eyes. "And call me if you need to talk. Friend to friend."

Some of the tension eased around his mouth, but he knew he'd never call. "Thanks, Nora." *For a whole lot of nothing I can make sense of.*

Three

From Pilar Valenzuela's journal, Monday, September 10:

It's great being able to choose what I want to do with my life from here on out. But sometimes it feels like I'm searching for something to replace my marriage. No class or book or hobby can do that.

But, wait. I don't want to think about Danny.

What can I write about MY life? I started yoga classes over at the community college, and I've been to one session. Being around all those students got me thinking about going back to school. Why not? I didn't mind working while Danny was getting his degree. We were always a team, and I did it willingly. To be honest, though, I did imagine I would get my chance later. (Damn, I brought up Danny again.)

I called Enrique, since he's working on a degree in non-profit management down at Metro State, and we discussed different schools and courses of study. I think I'd like Metro. Enrique says there are a lot of "nontraditional" students there (read: old), so I'd fit in!

Maybe I'll study English. I could be a teacher, or a writer. Or a book critic. (Haha.) Human services looked interesting, too. I could counsel women to be more assertive. You know what they say—those who can't, teach.

I wish I knew what Danny would think, but he probably wouldn't care. Wait. That's not fair. Danny always cared. Man, I'm really contradicting myself. (And, I brought up Danny again, damn it.)

This . . . sucks. And if that's the only description I can come up with, maybe English isn't the degree for me. Okay, to hell with it. I'm going to bring up Danny. I've never censored my journal entries before.

I can't get used to his conspicuous absence from the house. He wasn't home much before, but I could still feel his presence around, smell his cologne lingering in the air. I could see (trip over) his stuff. Now it really feels like he's gone. I wasn't prepared. Not in the slightest.

Every day I think of things to share with him, then I remember. He's gone. My choice. Is it ever gonna get easier?

The boys miss him, too. We've tried to be vague with them until we know what's gonna happen. We've explained that Danny is just keeping Uncle Ruben company for a while, but I can see in their eyes that they're worried. I don't want to keep Danny from them.

Here I go placating again. Terminally happy Pilar trying to keep the world spinning. UGH! Best case scenario? I want life to be just the way it's always been for the boys, but different for me.

Me<---impossible dreamer.

I'm a mess.

The phone rang as Pilar was gathering her workout gear for yoga class and stuffing it unceremoniously into the fuschia duffel she'd bought at Gart Sports the day before. She scowled at the phone on the second ring. The boys had dawdled and bickered before school, and now she was running late. No time to chat. On ring three, she admitted defeat and tucked the receiver between her ear and shoulder while whipping harried glances around the room. Where'd she put that damn mat?

"Hello?"

"Ah, *mi hijita.* You sound distracted. It's a bad time?"

Her mother-in-law. Pilar froze, her stomach plunging like the proverbial baby grand from the thirty-first floor. She hadn't expected Rosario's call so soon. Staggering to the nearest chair, Pilar sank into it, barely registering the pain when one of Teddy's pointy action figures gouged her thigh.

"H-hi, Rosario." The false cheer in her tone made her cringe. "I was, uh . . . actually, yeah. Headed out. But, I have a sec." She swallowed through a dread-tightened throat. "What's up?"

"No emergency, honey. You go on."

No emergency? How'd she figure? "No. I have time for you." Pilar shot a glance at her watch and winced. She respected Rosario too much to blow her off and had to get this horrible conversation over with sooner or later anyway.

"Just put my gorgeous son on," Rosario said with laughter in her voice. "I'm planning the annual Broncos versus Raiders family football party, but I can discuss it with Daniel. It's still a ways off. Go on."

She doesn't know.

The realization knocked the wind out of Pilar. She

struggled for words, unsure whether to be relieved or annoyed that Danny hadn't told his mother about the separation. But then again, she hadn't summoned the courage to call her own parents, either. She knew Mom would lecture her about her "wifely duty" to fix things with Danny, who was "such a good provider." Pilar couldn't stomach the "women make sacrifices, dear" speech again.

"Pilar? You still there?"

"Y-yes. Danny's . . . uh"—*think, Pilar!*—"not . . . up yet," she finished, taking the coward's route. "C-can I have him call you?"

"Not up yet?" Rosario sounded surprised.

Okay, so it was the stupidest excuse she could have concocted. Danny was a lifelong early riser. Lying sucked. "Swing shift got off late, so I let him sleep in."

Rosario murmured a sound of approval. "You're a good wife to my son, Pilar. And a good mama. They're lucky to have you."

The room swayed before Pilar's eyes. She squeezed them shut and pinched the bridge of her nose until it hurt, Rosario's words warring with those of her own mother. The praise was undeserved. A good wife didn't kick her husband out, now did she? A good wife worked things out, made things better, instead of letting them build and fester until they erupted. What could she possibly say to this woman who had loved her and accepted her from the very beginning?

The doorbell chimed, thank God, saving her the trouble of answering. Pilar shot to her feet. "Hang on. Someone's at the door."

"Okay, honey."

She could've kept talking on the cordless phone while she traversed the room, but instead used the reprieve to collect her thoughts. She fumbled with the dead bolt, then yanked the door open. *Danny*.

He held up one of Pep's textbooks, smiling though his eyes were wary. "I was in the neigh—"

Heart thudding, Pilar reached up and clapped her palm over his mouth. She tried to sound normal over the phone line. "Rosario! Sorry, it's UPS, so I have to go, but—oh, look! Danny just got up." Her desperate look begged him to go along. "Hold on. I'll let you talk to him."

Rosario clucked. "Oh, dear. I hope the phone didn't wake him after you took such pains to let him rest."

"N-no. It's okay." She covered the holes in the mouthpiece with her thumb and tugged Danny into the entryway with her free hand.

"Hurry up," she rasped. "It's your mom. She thinks—"

"You told her?" Danny paled.

"No, I said you were still sleeping." She raised a finger and gave him what she hoped was a stern look. "But, I don't like being cornered—"

"I'll talk to her, I promise. I just didn't know how to tell her without breaking her heart." Eyes wounded, he held out his hand and snapped his fingers toward his palm. Pilar relinquished the phone, fighting to dam up the flood of guilt his words had released.

As he stood talking in the foyer, Pilar wobbled back to the armchair, taking a moment to remove the nefarious action figure before she sat this time. Elbows on her knees, she furrowed her fingers into the front of her hair, and rested her forehead in her palms. Tension pounded behind her temples. This was more difficult than she'd ever imagined.

She hadn't considered Rosario.

Or the rest of the family, for that matter.

She'd imagined her marriage involved two people: her and Danny. Wrong. They'd been together so long, their lives and families were tightly woven, bound together in an intricate chain of love and time and promises. This would be painstaking, unraveling their lives without snapping all the threads in the process.

God, she didn't want to lose Rosario.

She thought of Pep and Teddy's round, cinnamon-scented Grandma V, and a painful lump rose in her throat. None of this was fair to the family. But should she sacrifice her own happiness just to keep the rest of her fragile world intact? Mom wouldn't hesitate to say yes, but Pilar disagreed. She'd done that enough already.

She listened to Danny stammer about the football party, selfishly grateful he was on the spot instead of her. Damn it, they needed to talk, make some plans so they wouldn't run into this again. Why were they dragging their feet? Couples separated every day. *Other couples. Not them.*

"Okay, Mama," Pilar heard him say, and she glanced up.

Mistake.

He looked freshly showered, the close-cropped black hair at his nape still damp. Well-faded jeans hugged his thighs and buttocks, emphasizing his taut strength and sleek muscularity. The off-white chambray shirt molded the width of his back, and the whole picture of this man she knew so well stole her breath. She knew the feel of those muscles from memory, the smell of his skin, the taste of him.

God, she loved his body. Loved *him*. Her mouth went dry from the unfulfilled yearning, and the leotard and sweatpants she'd donned felt suddenly too revealing. These days apart, the prospect of never being intimate with Danny Valenzuela again had jacked her libido into the triple-X range. She'd always found Danny's particular brand of masculinity impossible to resist.

Damn her for a traitor, *she wanted him*. Wanted to make love with him until their troubles faded, then curl into his chest and sleep against his steady heartbeat. The signals her body was giving were loud and clear.

As if she were throwing fistfuls of pheromones at him, he spun toward her and their eyes locked. His expression transformed from confusion to awareness with a subtle darkening. He'd always been able to read desire on her face . . . and elsewhere.

She crossed her arms over her chest indignantly. Although that telltale heat crawled up her flesh, she still couldn't tear her eyes away.

"I love you, too" he said into the receiver, his gaze never leaving Pilar's.

Enough! She jerked her attention away and rubbed the goose bumps on her arms, at odds with this bold rush of mixed emotions.

"I'll get back to you. Promise." A pause, and then in a lower, huskier tone. "I'll tell her. Bye."

He clicked off the phone and set it on the hall table. Thumbs tucked in the pockets of his jeans, he hung his head. An uncomfortable silence threatened to swallow them both. Pilar cleared her throat, and he looked up.

"T-tell me what?" Her voice sounded squawky. She watched his Adam's apple rise and fall.

"Mom wanted me to be sure to tell you how much I love and appreciate you." It almost sounded like an accusation.

"I didn't say anything to her."

"I know." With a sigh, he moved into the living room and sank onto the couch. Legs spread wide, he interlaced his fingers behind his head, leaned back, and stared at the ceiling. Pent up tension showed in the rhythmic bouncing of his heels. "God. I hate this, P."

She straightened the armrest covers with jerky motions. "Why haven't you told her yet? What if one of the boys had said something? I thought I was gonna die."

His head rolled to the side and he studied her. "Yeah? Well, I feel like I'm going to die a lot these days, so join the club." Another tense silence yawned. When he spoke again, his tone was lower. "I haven't told her because I hardly believe it myself. I don't want it to be true." There was no vehemence in his tone, just defeat. He closed his eyes. "I'm sorry if you can't understand that."

"I can." A sour feeling assailed her middle. "I-I

didn't mean to fly off. She just caught me by surprise."

"You and me both."

"We should talk about things, Danny. The boys. A-and, our families. There is a lot to be worked out." She stood. "C-can I get you anything? Have you eaten?"

"You don't have to wait on me, Pilar."

Her posture straightened. "I'll make coffee."

He glanced from her to the gym bag on the chair with her purse and keys. "Look, if I caught you on your way out—"

"No, this is more important and you're already here, so . . ." Pilar shrugged, then continued through the archway that led to the kitchen and breakfast nook. She spoke over her shoulder. "I'm too late for yoga class anyway. The boys were absolute demons this morning and I've been two steps behind ever since."

Ugh. Small talk. She couldn't bear it. She stood at the sink and filled the coffee carafe with cold water, staring out into the backyard. How strange to be merely *civil* to a man she'd loved since childhood. The sooner they could get past all this legal business and move on, the better. When she turned, he stood in the archway, studying her with his inscrutable deep brown eyes.

"You're taking yoga?" His gaze traced the scooped neckline of her royal blue leotard.

She ignored the suggestive trail of his eyes and suddenly noted the cut on his chin, held together with a butterfly bandage. Why hadn't she seen it before? Standing on tiptoe, she poured the water into the coffee machine. "What happened to your chin?"

Shoulder braced against the wall, he crossed his arms. "I had a car accident. When did you start taking yoga?"

The carafe hit the countertop with a clank. "An accident? When? In the Chevelle?" That car was his pride and joy.

"No." He rubbed his knuckles along his whisker-darkened jawline. "At work. Tell me about yoga."

She waved his persistent questions away, jangling the carafe into its spot on the warmer. "It's just a class, Danny. Something to do."

So. He'd crashed his car at work and no one thought to call her? She was still his wife, the mother of his sons, and she deserved—wait. She was acting like a territorial idiot. Nervous fingers lit on her temples before raking through her hair. *Stop it.*

But she couldn't. Jealousy's ugly, unnamed cousin took up residence below her breastbone, making her want to lash out. She took her time measuring coffee grounds into the filter and starting the brew cycle. When she felt able to speak calmly, she turned to him. Her gaze settled on his healing wound. "Why didn't you tell me, Danny?"

"Why didn't you tell me about yoga class?"

Her voice sharpened. "When was the last time you gave a single thought to how I spent my days or nights?"

Pain flashed over his face. "That's not fair, Pilar—"

"No, wait. Wait. You're right." She spun toward the sink and gripped the edge until her knuckles whitened, breathing deeply to regain her composure. "I don't want to fight. Honestly. We never fight—"

"Maybe that's not so good."

She heard the rustle of his jeans behind her.

"Maybe if you had vented, it wouldn't have come to this."

Was it true? Should she have hollered when she felt like it? Told him when things bothered her? She had been well-trained to smile sweetly and keep petty grievances and dirty laundry to herself, but her doubts about her mother's favorite lesson were mounting.

"I don't know. It's just . . ." She turned and shrugged helplessly. Her tone softened. "You had a car accident, and I didn't even know. I've known everything about you for the past seventeen years. It's just weird."

He spread his arms and looked around. "I don't live here anymore, remember? I didn't think you'd care that I had a little fender bender at work."

"Of course I care."

A tortured sound came from deep within him. "I don't understand what you want from me. Details about my life, or for me to get out of yours?"

God, she didn't want him out of her life. She wanted him back in her life . . . but the way it used to be. And that was impossible. Couldn't he see that?

She approached him and reached tentative fingers up to touch the bandage, careful to keep her voice neutral. "I care." She sniffed. "And I'm glad it was a patrol car and not the Chevelle. Stitches?"

"No." His tone was husky. Arms tensed at his sides,

he stood very still, watching her beneath his thick lashes. His breaths came slowly, measured.

She traced the small bandage again, aware of the runaway pulse in his muscular neck, the roughness of his whiskers on her fingertips. Some wild, idiotic part of her wanted to raise up on her toes and kiss him there, and on his throat, his chest, just to see if she could incite any kind of reaction. A weak voice inside urged her to invite him to bed for the day. So difficult to be near him and not want . . .

Don't do it, Pilar. It will only complicate things.

Her gaze flittered up to his eyes, and there she read confusion, pain—and desire, too. She was sending him mixed messages. Unfair. Clenching her jaw, she curled her fingers into her palm and pulled her hand back until it lay clutched against her chest. "I'm sorry."

"Don't be. I'm not." He wrapped one of her auburn curls around his finger, rubbing the strands with his thumb.

Easing away from him, she moved stiffly to the far end of the breakfast nook and took a seat, avoiding his eyes. Coffee gurgled, the only sound in the otherwise silent house. Its rich scent spiced the charged air, but when Pilar reached up to scratch her face, Danny's cologne on her fingers was all she could smell. What was happening to her?

"I'm thinking about college," she blurted, eager to obliterate the painful awareness crackling between them.

It took him a minute to reply, but thankfully, he followed her lead. "That's wonderful. You should go."

"Yeah?" She felt suddenly vulnerable. "It makes me nervous. I'll be older than everyone."

The corners of his mouth tipped down in sync with his "not a problem" shrug. "You have life experience. Don't devalue that." He chewed on the inside of his cheek for a moment, still standing in the archway. "You could have taken yoga or gone to college any time, P. You know that, right? I would have supported you."

She bit her lip. "I guess I wasn't ready until now." And perhaps that had been a mistake. If she'd had her own life, she might've held his attention.

"Did I hold you back?" he asked morosely.

She thought about it. "No."

"Because, if I did—"

"You didn't, Danny. I would tell you."

He expelled a caged breath. "God, I love you, Pilar."

Chest tight, she met his eyes across the room.

He shoved off the wall and stepped cautiously closer, as though trying to gauge her reaction. "I love you," he repeated, more passionately, "and I'll always love you. Whatever I did, I'm sor—"

"Danny . . . please don't."

"No." He tossed her plea aside with an impatient motion. "I have to say it. I want you to know."

She glanced over the countertop that separated the nook from the kitchen, chewing the insides of her cheeks to buy time before answering. "I love you, too. But, I can't live like this anymore, don't you see? *Damn it!*" Her voice cracked and she bit down good and hard to control the painful ache in her throat.

"Okay." His calm but intense voice soothed her. "I hear you, baby girl, loud and clear." He continued to advance on her, then squatted and took her hand in both of his, long, strong fingers massaging her knuckles as his words caressed her soul. "I may not have heard you before, but I do now. You have my undivided attention. If we love each other, we can find a way out of this together. God knows, I . . . I want you to be happy. It's all I've ever wanted."

It sounded good, but giving in would mean settling. Again. After a brief "honeymoon," things would turn lonely again and she'd be stuck. She shored up her resolve. "If you want me to be happy, th-then you have to go."

The caresses stopped. He looked away. After a long pause, his ravaged eyes swung back to meet hers. She saw moisture there, which shocked her. Like her, Danny hardly ever cried. Such paragons of control.

"Me leaving would make you happy?"

She shrugged one shoulder, desperation swelling inside her. "I don't . . . it's all I know to do at this point."

His lips pressed into a hard line, then he pushed to his feet and claimed the chair across from her. He settled his elbows on Teddy's Batman placemat, looking tired . . . and so bleak. "You tell me what you want from me, then."

Her words came in a jumbled rush. "I don't want us to be enemies, Danny. I'm tired of being angry. What's done is done. For the boys' sake—"

"Pilar." He splayed his hands across his chest.

"Haven't you heard a word I've said? I could never be your enemy. I. Love. You."

She smiled sadly at him. So easy for him to say now. What about the past several years, when he'd gotten so wrapped up in his work that he'd rarely even smiled? Burning questions begged to be asked. What'd she have to lose? "Why haven't you touched me? Why haven't we made love in so long?"

His brows dipped, and he blinked in confusion. "B-because you had no interest, obviously."

Oh, now it was her fault. "You're so sure?"

He spread his arms wide. "I may not be Mr. Intuition, but there are things I do understand. Your signals were pretty damn clear."

"Maybe you were misreading them. Maybe it hurt that you didn't make love to me." She leaned closer across the small table. "Did you ever ask, or try?"

"Did *you?*" He reached over and grabbed her upper arm gently. "Why couldn't you just tell me what you needed? When was the last time *you* came on to me?" He let his eyes wander down her body. "When was the last time you showed me anything but cold distance, Punky? I'm not a mind reader."

Esme's identical words rushed into her mind, and guilt cracked down like a judge's gavel on her head. Feeling exasperated and unsure, she sighed, tangling her fingers in her hair. "It's not just . . . the sex. I shouldn't have brought that up. F-forget it."

"I don't want to forget it." His thumbs moved in slow, intoxicating circles on her arm. "If it's lovemaking you want, baby girl, then we're on the same page. Believe me. Say the word and I'll take you upstairs and show you how much I love you, how much I want—"

"Stop." She wrenched away, jerking her palms toward him stiffly. "Just stop. It's moved beyond that. I don't want you to make love to me to prove a point."

A sound of masculine indignation pushed up from inside him, and Pilar knew he wasn't going to let the disturbing seductive talk drop. God, she wished he would.

"It wouldn't be to prove anything. It would—"

"Danny, please—"

"—be two people who love each other, who want—"

"No more!" she interjected, unable to hear another word about lovemaking. It hurt too much. Making love wouldn't cure their problems, and she couldn't bear the sensual pain the topic conjured.

She sighed, pressing two fingers to the sharp pain in her forehead. Her eyes drifted closed. "What I want is to figure out how we're going to tell our families. How we'll handle time with the boys. That's what we should be discussing. Not making love, please—"

"Okay," he barked, and her face lifted. His expression told her he immediately regretted the harshness of the word.

Gritting his teeth, he took a moment to still the taut air between them, the muscle in his temple jumping. "Okay," he said again, softer. "I'm sorry. But, hear me when I say I don't want this. I want our life back. And I *want* you," he added pointedly. "I've wanted you since sophomore English class. Believe it."

She stood and moved past him into the kitchen,

preparing their coffee with wooden motions. His eyes burned into her, but she concentrated on her task, on slowing her pounding heart. On ignoring what he insisted on telling her.

I want you.

She carried the mugs back to the table and set one in front of him with a decisive clunk, determined to stay on track. "What are we going to do about the get-together at your mom's?" Did he truly want to make love to her right now? Desire swirled hot and low within her. "You could tell her you have to work. She'd believe that."

His wistful gaze had settled on the family photos above the buffet, and she tracked it. The boys as babies, school pictures, a family photo—and her favorite candid wedding shot, laughing just after she'd shoved cake in his face. . . .

"She'd still want you and the boys there."

"True." She'd have to put the wedding picture away.

"Besides, she knows I'm on vacation." Danny scrubbed his palm over his face.

Bitterness flared inside Pilar, and she turned her attention from the photo wall. "You never take a vacation."

He sipped his coffee. "Well, after the crash, my supervisor strongly suggested I get my head together. That or a visit to the department shrink, probably." His lips twisted ruefully. "Eh, what the hell? It's been too long since I've taken time off, anyway."

No kidding. She wanted to ask why they hadn't enjoyed more family vacations. Why they hadn't stolen a weekend now and then to rekindle the flames that used to burn so hot between them. She didn't ask, but the kernel of resentment wouldn't disappear. "How long will you be off?"

"Open-ended. I guess that depends . . ."

Surely it didn't depend on her. Danny Valenzuela didn't let garden-variety emotions like heartbreak interfere with his tunnel-visioned work ethic. "So, what about the football party?"

He quirked one eyebrow. "We could just go. The boys would love it. What could it hurt?"

"Danny." Her tone was droll but tender. "We can't lie. We have to tell her. All of them."

A little ray of hope fizzled in his eyes, turning them dull and flat. "Fine, P, I'll tell them. I'll tell everyone that we're just another sad family statistic."

She lifted her chin, refusing to let him goad her into an argument. "Do that. The sooner the better."

He drank, watching her over the cup's rim, then wiped his lips. "What's the next step in your grand plan to reach the greener grass on the other side?"

Her spine bristled, but she forged ahead. "Divorce mediation." Her hands tightened around her mug. "It's cheaper than lawyers and puts the interests of the children fir—"

"Jesus, Pilar." He shot to his feet, stalked to the doorway, then turned back. "You've got this whole thing scheduled and booked, don't you? How long have you been planning to leave me?"

"Danny . . ."

"An opportunity to make things better . . ." He held up a finger, sarcasm lacing his words. "A single second chance to save two decades of love would've been downright considerate of you."

"I'm trying to make things easier, not harder."

He braced one hand high on the doorjamb. A muscle in his strong, square jaw ticked. "We haven't been apart a month yet, and you're talking divorce. What's easy about that?"

She crossed to him. "Why prolong the agony?"

His disbelieving expression caved into resignation. "Fine. Mediation. But for the record, separating children from a father who loves them *isn't* in their best interest." He knocked the side of his fist on the wall twice before turning to leave.

Her heart thumped. She didn't want him to leave with bad feelings. "Danny—!"

He whirled back. "Oh, yeah. One last thing." In a single, powerful stride, he stood right before her, his chest at her eye level.

She peered up at him. His nostrils flared and he paused only briefly before reaching around to smooth one hand against the small of her back and drive the other one into the side of her hair. He pressed her against his body. His gaze touched her lips first, but his mouth was quick to follow.

The kiss attacked like a Rocky Mountain zephyr wind, unexpected and all-encompassing, leaving her disoriented and breathless. His tongue controlled her mouth, caressing, tasting, probing. He molded her curves against his hard body, the not-so-subtle grinding of his hips a striking reminder of their earlier discussion.

Her limbs felt heavy and numb, and her body

readied for him in a flash of heat and moisture. So starved for his touch, she didn't even think of pulling away until he already had. As he released her, she stumbled forward, stunned to see him widening the distance between them.

"W-what are you doing?" The words were a gasp.

"Leaving. Because that's what will make you happy. And, though you may not believe it, everything I have ever done, wrong or right, Pilar, was to make you happy."

He turned. The back of his hand went gently to his mouth, but his eyes never left her face. When he spoke, his voice was husky with sexual desire. "I wanted to make love to you, P, all those months. I ached with it. Still do." As if to emphasize his point, he glanced down at his body, then back at her. "I'm only sorry I didn't when I had the chance."

He didn't let her respond, and Pilar jumped when the door slammed, squeezing her eyes shut. She sank to the floor and tucked her knees to her chest. Her skin hummed and her brain buzzed. She wanted to hurt, but couldn't feel a thing.

She had never been more confused in her life.

Four

Voice mail message from Pilar for Danny, left on his brother Ruben's answering machine, Friday, September 14:

"Hi Danny, and, uh, Ruben. It's Pilar. Anyway, Danny, I made an appointment with the mediator. Monday morning, ten o'clock. Unless I hear otherwise, I expect you'll be there. Just, um, meet me in the office. The address is on that paperwork I sent. Thanks. Bye."

An unsent letter from Dan Valenzuela to Pilar, dated Saturday, September 15:

Dear Punky:

You've been avoiding me for almost a week now, ever since we kissed. I understand you want space. I'm trying to respect that, but it's not easy.

I got your message, but I want you to know something. I agreed to go only because you're holding all the cards. I'm afraid if I say no, you'll serve me with divorce papers so fast my head will spin. I don't want to go, P. Mediation sessions, lawyers—anything that brings me closer to losing you forever is a bad idea in

*my book. I'm not ready to give up on us. I'll never be
ready.*

*Look, things went sour. Okay? I see now how wrong
I was to think that ignoring the tension would make it
go away. And, yes, I sensed it, but I didn't know what
to do. You never even gave me a warning. I can apologize until my throat's sore and make promises you'll
never believe, but where will that get me?*

*I'm gonna make things right between us. Somehow.
I'll win you back if it kills me; I just have to find a
way. We belong together, baby girl. I cannot bear the
thought of life without you. I love you. So much.*

*God, who am I kidding? I can't send this. You'd
just fight me harder if you read it.*

Damn, Punky. . . .

I always did love your fire.

Dan pulled into Ruben's cracked driveway at
eight-thirty on Monday morning, looking, feeling,
and probably smelling like roadkill. He'd spent a tu-
multuous weekend wasting tanks of gas and sleeping
in his car, feeling so desperate and heartsick, he
couldn't face Ruben or anyone.

It began as aimless driving, sucking up pavement
and waiting for the pain to subside. But around dusk
on Saturday, it occurred to him that he'd systemati-
cally visited all the old haunts that jogged happy
memories about Pilar.

He traced the route he had used to walk her
home from school. He parked by the weeping wil-
low in old Harold Fitzmiller's yard—the site of his
and Pilar's first kiss. It had tasted like bubble gum

lip gloss and felt like heaven, and even though Pilar had giggled during the most serious moment in his life up to that point, he'd never recovered. She'd ensnared him with her velvet laugh and one sweet kiss.

He lunched at the pizza joint where they'd go after football games, remembering those stolen back-booth kisses that made his teammates cup hands around their mouths and holler, "Get a room, Valenzuela!" Pilar had always hated that.

As darkness fell, he drove to the secluded parking spot overlooking the Denver skyline where they'd first made love. In a car. Such a cliché, but damn, what a memory. They were just kids then, the summer before their senior year. Too young to be making love, but too blinded by emotion to refrain. The Pope himself couldn't have kept them apart that sultry July night. The moon had been their candlelight, the crickets their music. Afterward, Danny knew his life's goal was to marry Pilar and make love to her until the day he died.

Parked in their spot, Dan reclined his seat and allowed memories of Pilar smiling up at him through her tears that night to flood him. He felt her shaky fingers tracing his lips, heard her tremulous voice whispering, "I love you, Danny Valenzuela. Forever and a day."

And then he wept for all the magic he so desperately didn't want to lose. Pilar may not have a tear to shed over him, but he had a river of them for her.

His grief spent, he wrote her the letter, then realized he couldn't send it. So he'd slept until Sunday morning, then filled the day with more of the same. Now, after five hundred miles of wear and tear on the Chevelle's tires and two nights sleeping cramped behind the wheel, he resigned himself to the damnable mediation meeting. He couldn't see another option. Even the wildest horse could only buck so long before breaking.

Dan wrenched out of the Chevelle, groaning as he straightened. He let himself in the kitchen door off the side of the house. Ruben, his oldest brother at 39 and the only divorced one out of the five, sat hunkered over the table eating Cocoa Krispies and scanning the newspaper. Katie Couric chattered in the background, a boxed American smile to keep lonely people company in the morning.

Ruben glanced up. His thick brows dipped. "The hell you been, Dan?"

"Nowhere." Dan rustled up a mug and filled it with his brother's lethal brew. "Driving. Trying not to lose my mind." Glancing over his shoulder, Dan noticed his brother wasn't wearing his usual construction site attire of jeans, a T-shirt, and steel-toed boots. As the owner of a small but growing concrete contracting company, he usually worked six on, one off. So why the sweats and slippers on a Monday?

Dan gave a jerk of his chin. "What's the deal—you off today?"

"Yeah. Waiting on permits, but those jokers from the county are sitting on their hands. I won't mention where their thumbs are." He shook his head. "No sense paying the guys to play Old Maid for eight hours. What about you?"

"Off until further notice. Obermeyer doesn't want me back until I get my life worked out."

Ruben snorted. "That'll be the day."

One corner of Dan's mouth lifted. His brother had been really patient with his brooding silence. He owed him an explanation. "You mind sticking around while I shower?" Dan walked toward the basement stairs. "I need to talk."

"No prob. I'll be here and all ears." Ruben indicated the answering machine with a disinterested flick of his spoon. "You have some messages."

"Okay." Dan took a tentative sip of the black, bitter coffee his brother revered, and grimaced. "Shower first, messages later. I can't stand myself a moment longer."

"I second that emotion, bro."

Half an hour later, Dan emerged from the basement feeling like a new man—at least on the outside. In deference to the meeting with Pilar, he wore brown Dockers and a green, navy, and brown plaid shirt she'd bought him last Christmas. As promised, Ruben still sat at the table, engrossed in the crossword puzzle. He looked up, the edge of the paper rustling in his hand.

"What's a five-letter word for postulate?"

"Hell if I know." Dan pointed at his mug. "You mind if I make a fresh pot? This motor oil is apt to kill us both."

"Go for it. Wuss. But if it looks like herbal tea or tastes like French vanilla, you're dead. Fair warning."

Dan smirked, then crossed to the cupboard, hunting for the filters and grounds.

Ruben tapped the tip of his pencil on the paper. "You had another call, too."

Dan looked from the machine to his brother, hope blowing through him like soap bubbles. "Pilar?"

"Nope."

Then he didn't care. He set his jaw and turned to his task with a new heaviness in his chest. What did he think? Pilar'd suddenly have a change of heart and beg him back? About as likely as him coming up with a five-letter word for "postulate" off the top of his head.

After setting the pot to brew, Dan walked to the table and pulled out a chair with his foot. He sank down and raked his fingers through his hair, then regarded Ruben over the annoyingly cheery cereal box. Of all his brothers, Ruben might understand his plight. His wife, Merrilee, had left him two years earlier because he "didn't communicate." Whatever happened to the appeal of the strong, silent type?

Ruben had persevered through the pain, but Dan had noticed his stoic brother had been even quieter since Merrilee had shattered his world. The Valenzuela men were all too tenderhearted for their own damn good.

His eyes focused on the puzzle spread out before him. Ruben sniffed. "I'm listening, Dan."

"She kicked me out."

Ruben's crossword concentration didn't waver, but he nodded sagely. "Not a news flash, bro, since you've been camped on the hide-a-bed from hell for two weeks. Didn't entertain any illusions that I'd suddenly become more fun than L'il Bit. Does Mom know?"

"Not yet."

Ruben's brows flicked up and back down. "You hope."

"What do you mean?"

His brother hiked one meaty shoulder. "Mom's pretty sharp. Can't pull too much over on her. I would've thought you learned that back in high school." He thrust his chin forward, scratching the fleshy underside with nonchalance.

Dan blew out a tired breath. "I can't make myself believe it's true, Rube. I keep thinking Pilar will come to her senses. Mom was so angry with Merrilee. I don't want that to happen with Pilar. They get along so well."

Ruben blinked at him. "Which is why you oughtta tell her before she hears it from my nephews or tricks me into spilling it. That'd hurt her, you and L'il Bit keeping it from her like that." His eyes dropped to the puzzle. "Just a suggestion. You gotta do what feels right."

"Going home would feel right." Dan paced to the coffeemaker and filled his mug. Turning back, he leaned against the counter and braced his hands on the edge, spread wide. He crossed one ankle over the other. "I don't want to lose my family. Telling Mom makes it . . . more real."

The chair legs squeaked beneath Ruben's stocky form as he leaned back. "Take it from me—denial won't make it go away."

Dan knew he was right. "Want to know the worst part? I've known something was bothering Pilar for months, maybe longer." He tried to smile through his chagrin, but only one half of his mouth cooperated. "Thought if I ignored it, things would improve."

Ruben's eyes looked baleful in his round face. "I hear you, brother. Like a friggin' echo."

"Yeah." All his brothers lived nearby, but he hadn't thought twice before coming to Ruben's. He wrapped cold fingers around the warm mug and returned to his seat. "What should I do?"

"My honest opinion?" Ruben leaned in, his tone adamant. "Fight for her, Dan. Whatever it takes, whatever you have to sacrifice, go the distance." He pointed one thick finger. "Don't give up or back down, or you'll regret it for the rest of your life." His older brother's chubby face fell.

Dan ached for him. "You miss her, Rube?"

"Constantly. If I had just one more chance to get her back, I'd blabber on till I lost my voice. But I don't." He paused. "You still have a chance with Pilar. Don't let it slip away."

Dan shook his head slowly. "How'd we wind up like this?"

Ruben pursed his lips, thinking. "You're the youngest. I'm the oldest. For whatever reason, I think we took what happened between Mom and Victor more to heart than Tony, Frank, and Randy did, and it shaped us in certain ways."

"And that's bad?" Danny shrugged. "I thought I'd learned from Victor's mistakes so I wouldn't repeat them."

Ruben lumbered up from his chair and got a cup of coffee. "We didn't repeat his, bro. We made our own. Hell, I hold everything inside. You're a workaholic—"

"You think I'm a workaholic?" Dan frowned.

Ruben's droll glance had "duh" written all over it.

Dan traced his finger over a scratch in the oak tabletop and considered this. "Huh. I never thought of myself that way. After how Victor left Mom, I never wanted that kind of heartache to touch my family. So I work hard because I know it's what he *wouldn't* have done."

"Rationalize it all you want, but it doesn't change the fact you're a workaholic." Ruben hooked one foot over the other. "Victor is a big part of the men we turned out to be, Dan, like it or not."

The thought made Dan sick. He hated to wonder if he'd driven his wife away in a blind attempt to keep her. He glanced at the clock, uncomfortable with the direction the conversation had taken. "I've got to hit it. But . . ."

"Spit it out."

"Suppose I fight so hard that it only pushes her farther away?"

Ruben looked at him for a long time, just shaking his head. "What've you got to lose? You're at rock bottom, buddy. Claw your way up or lie there and die, your choice. I'm just experience talking, and"— he indicated the liberal gray shot through his black hair—"it ain't pretty."

The phone rang. "You get it," Ruben said, pushing off the counter. "Damn thing never rang until you started shacking here."

Dan smiled as he stood. "You know I appreciate you listening, everything."

"I just hope some of it got through." Ruben

reached over and knocked on Dan's head. "Aside from being a workaholic, you're also pretty thick." He jerked his chin toward the phone as it rang a third time. "And I'm not your damn social secretary, little brother. Answer the phone."

Dan watched his brother leave the room and scooped it up on ring four. "Hello?"

"Dan? It's Nora." Her voice held notes of relief and exasperation. "Why haven't you called me back?"

"Nora, I—" he glanced at the clock. He hadn't figured work would call during his vacation. "I was gone all weekend. Just got in. What's up?"

"Where was your pager? Your cell? No, forget it. You're on vacation. Have you forgotten what today is?"

Today? He leaned his hip against the counter and hooked the phone cord on his elbow. Hmmm, well, it was Monday. Possibly the first day of the end of his marriage, but she wouldn't call for . . . September 17 . . . damn! Urgency jerked him to attention. He back-hammered his fist against the cupboard door. "The sergeant's test. I completely forgot—"

"Well, don't stand there stammering. Get your ass in the car and blaze down to headquarters. If you don't take it today, you can't take it again until next year."

"But—"

"You want the promotion or not? I'll meet you there with your paperwork. Leave now or you'll never make it."

He couldn't reply.

"Dan?"

War waged inside his heart and mind. Granted, he

didn't want to wait until next year. He'd been studying for the difficult test for months. Then again, he had an appointment to meet with Pilar and the mediator. . . .

An appointment to end his marriage.

The realization struck him like an uppercut, leaving him dazed with its wrongness. He was surrendering way too easily, exactly what Ruben had warned against. He didn't *want* to start the process of divorce, be it mediation or obtaining lawyers. He didn't dare take even one step toward that unfathomable end.

Don't give up or back down, or you'll regret it for the rest of your life.

His fist clenched. Ruben was right. Dan had to fight Pilar's "why prolong the agony?" excuse. She was running scared, that's all. They had so many opportunities to work things out before it came to divorce, and he wouldn't back down until he convinced her of that.

Resolute, he set his jaw. "I'll meet you there. Just let me grab my cell phone. I need to make a call on the way."

"I'm sorry to make you drive down here. I just didn't know what to do." Truthfully, Pilar couldn't summon the energy to get in her car and drive away. Instead, she and Esme sat huddled in uncomfortable chairs in the stark waiting room of the mediation offices.

"Don't apologize." Esme adjusted position in the

chair and grimaced. "Even beached whales need to get out of the house now and then."

Pilar flashed a guilty glance at her very pregnant friend. "How are you feeling?"

"Better than you, at this point."

Murderers on death row probably felt better than she did right now. "I can't believe he didn't show. After all this." She twisted her wrist, then let her hand drop in her lap.

Ever the logical one, Esme said, "Listen, don't fly off until you know the circumstances. I'm sure something just came up, sweetie."

Pilar spread her arms. "But don't you see? Something *always* just comes up. Something else is always more important than me and this marriage, and I'm forever forced to give in."

Esme quirked her mouth to the side. Pilar didn't envy her the position of designated sympathizer—nothing could soothe this ache.

"You want to know the worst part?" Pilar's self-derisive laugh held no humor. "Last week, he came over and he kissed me." She flashed Esme an assessing glance, but read no judgment in her gaze. "I've spent the last week second-guessing my decision. I had almost convinced myself that Danny *had* seen the light, that we might be able to work this marriage out. I was planning to talk to him after this appointment. I'm pathetic."

Esme's expression shone with encouragement. "Pilar, you still can work it out. If you guys clear the air, and—"

"No." Pilar stood and hiked her purse up on her

shoulder. "Whatever stupid romantic thoughts I had are gone. This was it. If he can't even bother to show when our marriage is on the line, forget it. I don't need Danny Valenzuela, and I refuse to smile and make nice anymore." She spun and headed for the double doors before Esme recognized the crushing disappointment on her face.

He hadn't reached Pilar before he'd run out the door and headed for police headquarters. She must have left early. The machine picked up, and he opened his mouth . . . but nothing emerged. He'd worried she would misconstrue whatever he said, no matter the explanation, so he'd hung up without speaking. But as his heels struck the sidewalk leading to police headquarters, he doubted himself. He had a well-developed cop's gut after eleven years on patrol, and every instinct inside him screamed, "Mistake!" But he was here now. Might as well follow through.

He dragged his wallet out of his back pocket and flashed his badge at the deputy manning the metal detectors before shouldering through the arch. That nagging feeling of doom chased him through the lobby and into the long, wood-paneled hallway, warning him he shouldn't be here. He should be with Pilar. *Too late.*

"Dan!"

He whirled back as Sgt. Obermeyer rushed to catch him. She wore jeans and a sweatshirt, a manila folder clutched beneath her arm.

Her eyes flashed with annoyance as she neared.

"I called your name about five times. Didn't you hear me?"

He peered over her shoulder to the austere lobby he'd plowed blindly—and apparently deafly—through. "Sorry. I guess I wasn't paying attention."

She shuffled through the folder and whipped out a form. Her eyes traced the text briefly before she held it out to him. He hardly spared it a glance before folding it into quarters and shoving it in his back pocket.

Nora shook her head, peering up at him quizzically. "I can see vacation hasn't done you much good. Are you even ready to take this test?"

"I've studied." He rubbed his knuckles along his jawline.

"Dan . . . what's going on?" She glanced at her watch, and he followed suit. Still a couple of minutes before the test would start, but more than half an hour late for mediation. He toyed with the idea of finding a quiet corner and pulling out his cell phone. But what could he say to Pilar now, after the fact? I made *another* mistake? Forgive me, *again*?

"Dan!"

He frowned and shook his head as if to clear the daze. "I'm sorry." He moved aside to let a group of plainclothes officers pass, then leaned against the wall, blowing a breath out pursed lips. "I think I really screwed up."

"Why? What happened?" She crossed her arms, the folder dangling from one hand.

"Pilar scheduled a mediation appointment for us today. I'd forgotten about the test so . . . after you called, I couldn't reach her to tell her I couldn't make it, and now—"

"Oh, no." Nora's face fell. "But the test shouldn't take you too long. What time's the appointment?"

"It *was* at ten."

"Wait a sec—you blew it off?" Her eyes grew round with dismay. "You blew off a chance to . . . for a stupid promotional test?" She released a short, incredulous laugh. "Did you hear nothing I told you in the office that night?"

"I heard, but my brother—" Damn, wrong choice. Ruben had said fight *for* her, not fight *with* her. He spread his arms and shrugged, a feeling of utter ineptitude hitting him like a blast of pepper spray to the face. "What now?"

"You have to ask? I should knock you upside the head." She grabbed a fistful of his sleeve and propelled him toward the exit without letting go. "Go to your wife, Dan. Go! The job, promotions—none of it matters more than family. . . ."

"I know that, but—"

"No buts," she barked. "*Never* make the mistake of putting the job first."

Nora was right. He'd thought he was putting his family first *by* putting the job first, but he'd been wrong. He picked up speed as they reached the metal detectors. They passed through one after the other, leaving the building at a jog. Nora followed him as far as the threshold before stopping. "Good luck!" she called. "You damned annoying male!"

* * *

Damn hindsight and its twenty-twenty vision. The very concept bugged the hell out of him. The entire drive from police headquarters to Pilar's house—his house—Dan kicked himself. Based on everything she'd told him since the split, all the things that had made her unhappy, how could he have thought for a moment that skipping the mediation appointment would be a wise strategic move? He banged his fist against the steering wheel and swore.

By the time he pulled in behind her car, desperation had taken hold of his brainwaves, and he didn't even think he'd be able to explain the convoluted thought processes that had led him to make the wrong decision. But he had to try.

He straightened his shirt, then strode with more confidence than he felt toward the door. Esme's car he noted, sat next to Pilar's, the engine still ticking. That could be bad. He rang the bell twice, then stood back and prayed. His throat closed when the dead bolt slid home, but it was Esme's face, not Pilar's, that peered out. Relief showed in her eyes, then she eased out, closing the door behind her. "I don't think she'll talk to you. What happened, Dan?"

"Damn it." He clenched everything, then released it. "It was . . . a work issue, but it doesn't matter. I should've blown it off and been there for Pilar."

Esme crossed her arms atop her distended belly. Her tone gently chastised, but her eyes looked almost sympathetic. "Maybe not blown it off, but you should've tried to make other arrangements, or at least said something to Pilar."

But, but, but! his mind defended, though logic told him his argument sucked. "I called, but . . . damn it." He smoothed his palm down his face. "My excuses sound lame even to me, Esme. I don't want to waste your time or insult your intelligence rattling them off. I was an ass."

A wan smile lifted one side of her mouth. "Well, at least you two agree on something. She's talking about serving papers, speaking to you only through lawyers. I'm trying to calm her and make her less reactive, but . . ." She shrugged.

Through his haze of worry, he heard her words and did a double take. "You aren't pro-divorce?"

She socked him in the shoulder, but softened it with a wink. "Don't be a bonehead, Dan. Who else but Pea would put up with an annoying guy like you?"

One half of his mouth cooperated with his feeble attempt at a smile. This was good, having Esme on his side. He needed her to understand how desperately contrite he felt about the appointment, but the only words that came to mind were, "I don't want anyone but her. Ever."

"I know." Esme tilted her head to the side. "But I'll be honest. It doesn't look good."

Dan cupped her elbows and hunkered down until their eyes were level. "Es, I beg you. Convince her to let me explain. I just want to tell her what was going on in my brain when I made the decision to go to work instead of meeting her. I screwed up. I don't expect forgiveness—"

"Good thing."

"I'll leave her alone for a while, give her some space after this if she'll just . . . listen."

Esme cast him a dubious look. "I'll try, but no promises. You know how stubborn she can be. Give me a sec." She tossed him a playfully stern glare. "And don't make any other guy-brain decisions while you wait, okay?"

He pointed down. "I'm frozen to this spot."

She disappeared into his house, and he leaned against the wrought-iron railing that edged the small concrete stoop. Frozen was a weak description of how he felt. Numb. Dead, even. He didn't move. Hardly breathed. He merely waited, trying to clear his mind and praying she would see him.

After several minutes, Pilar's stony face peered around the edge of the door, and he cast up a silent vote of sainthood for Esme. He couldn't imagine how she'd convinced Pilar to listen to him.

Anger flashed beneath the utter disappointment he read in Pilar's closed expression. "What?" Her tone was pure ice.

He pushed off the railing, but words failed him even more dismally than he'd failed her. How in the hell did a man say the right thing in this situation? *State the obvious. It's a start.* Moistening his lips with a nervous flick of his tongue, he took the plunge. "I made a terrible mistake."

Her hard expression didn't change.

Flipping his hands helplessly, he forged on. "Pilar, I'll tell you right now, this won't sound reasonable to you. But . . . if you could put yourself into my mindset, just for a minute. Please." When she didn't slam the door, as he'd expected, he lowered his head, shifting his weight foot to foot while he planned his next words.

"I've been ravaged since you left the message about mediation. Shredded. But I planned on being there." He enunciated slowly. "I really did."

Her lashes fluttered, but she lifted her chin.

"Then, this morning, Nora called me at Ruben's. I haven't mentioned this, but I've been studying to take the sergeant's test for six months. It was today."

"Why didn't you call me on Friday, then?" Her voice sounded croaky and accusatory. She cleared her throat. "I even gave you an out to reschedule."

"I didn't call because I'd forgotten about the test." He clasped his hands together at chest level, gesturing gently with them. "My only thoughts, sweetheart, have been about you and me. I didn't remember until Nora called me, right about the time I was heading out the door to meet you."

"But you didn't come meet me." Her words were judge, jury, and executioner, and just like that he was a dead man walking.

A thick pause ensued. "No. But I called."

"There wasn't a message."

"I"—he made a sound of disgust—"didn't know what to say without making you angry."

"So you said nothing." It wasn't a question. Scorn moved over her face. "That's just perfect. Anything else?"

"Yes. Remember, think like me." He combed impatient fingers through his hair. "I chose the test because I got it into my head that agreeing to mediation was as good as telling you I'm okay with the divorce. Which I'm not."

She didn't so much roll her eyes as let them drift heavenward and back down.

Chagrin spread through him. She wasn't swayed. "I know, it's stupid. *Now,* I know. But, with that in my head, I drove to headquarters instead of meeting you."

Her head jerked to the side in a stiff shrug. "Well, I guess I know what really matters to you, Danny." She started to close the door. "Enjoy your promo—"

"Wait." He smacked his palm against the door, urgency bringing his words out faster. "Let me finish. I didn't take the test, Punky. That's what I'm telling you. I know it's too little, too late, and I missed the appointment regardless. But, I'm learning. I'm trying, baby girl. I don't care if I have to wait until next year to go for the promotion, or if I never get it. I love you."

She blinked rapidly then dropped her gaze. "Is that all?"

"I love you. That's not all, that's a lot." He waited, but she didn't look at him. It was his most dreaded standoff realized. Him on the outside of their life looking in, her closed expression saying he'd never be welcome inside again. He'd almost decided to admit defeat and walk away when her soft voice stopped him.

"The thing is, Danny, it always takes you until after the fact to remember your family. Don't you see that?"

His mouth opened, but he couldn't dispute her point. *Perception is reality.* Nora had reminded him, Pilar's perspective was the only one that truly mattered this time. It wouldn't help to explain that his awkward way of showing love was working, taking care of her. But couldn't she at least see how desperately he wanted to change? To be the kind of husband she needed? He blew out a defeated breath. "I hear you, but—"

"Because I see us being last on your priority list. I feel it, too, and it hurts like hell." Her regretful gaze pulled to his. "It wasn't supposed to be like this, Danny. I don't want to hurt anymore."

Emotion clogged his throat as he clenched and unclenched his fists, desperate to grasp what was slipping away. He reached for her, but she shook her head and his fingers folded into his palm.

His torment must have shown on his face, because Pilar sighed. "Don't give me that look. I don't hate you. But I'm not ready to forgive you for this, either. Can you understand that?"

"Yes," he whispered hoarsely. "But I'm not ready to throw in the towel on this marriage. Can *you* understand that?"

"I understand that *you're* not. But you'll have to keep the faith for both of us at this point, Danny, because I don't see anything but the end." She lifted her chin. "I'm sorry you missed the test. I know how important it must've been for you."

"Nothing is as important as you."

"Words, Danny. Pretty, empty words. That's all you keep giving me, and it's not enough." With that, the door snicked shut on his house and in his heart.

* * *

Pilar pressed her back against the door and squeezed her eyes shut. "Damn him," she whispered.

"Don't tell me you can't see how desperately that guy loves you, Pea!"

Emotion socked her in the gut. "I've already told you, Es, sometimes love isn't enough."

Esme brushed back a lock of hair that had tangled to Pilar's eyelashes. "And I'm telling *you*, sometimes it is enough, if you can find it in your heart to forgive and move on." She paused, her face a mask of sympathy and understanding. "Can't you remember what made you love Danny in the first place?"

"Ignorance? Youth?"

"No." Esme ticked qualities off on her slim fingers. "He was a hard worker, dependable. Always went the extra mile. He made you feel secure, you told me—"

"So?" Esme frowned. "That was then and this is now."

"I disagree. He may be taking things to extremes these days, but he still goes the extra mile. He's that same dependable hard worker—"

"Yeah," Pilar interjected, "but he used to go the extra mile for me, not for his work. And I don't feel secure anymore. I feel forgotten. Critical difference."

Esme sighed. "Well, he seems willing to work on it. Desperate to, actually."

Pilar pushed off the door and scuffed into the living room. She flung her body back on the couch. "I thought you were on my side."

"I am, geek. Which is why I don't want to see you throw away a life you've worked so hard to build, with a man who is truly your soul mate. No one ever promised it would be easy." She spread her arms wide. "Face it, men are organically annoying. It's what the Y chromosome truly stands for. '*Why* am I infuriating? *Why*, I'm a man! What else?' "

Pilar laughed grudgingly.

"But they have good qualities, too. You just have to ask yourself"—Esme picked up their mugs and headed toward the kitchen—"is it worth it?"

Pilar gnawed her lip and pondered this, coming up blank. Leave it to Esme to ask profound yet unanswerable questions. Jamming her arms crossed, she frowned. "Well?" she yelled toward the kitchen. "Is it?"

Esme didn't respond.

Five

From Pilar Valenzuela's journal, Monday, September 24:

I had planned to attend back-to-school night alone, but I got a voice mail from Danny, and he said he'd meet me there. I'm not holding my breath. I'm still angry with him over the mediation thing, but of course, in moments when I'm not feeling totally self-centered, I hope he does show up for the boys' sake. Husband and wife or not, we're still their parents. If we can't act like adults and pull it together long enough to stay involved in Pep and Teddy's lives, well, that's just pathetic. I'm adamant that this divorce will not affect the boys.

And . . . okay. Maybe I want to see him just a tiny bit. Call me a hypocrite, but I wonder how he's doing after our huge argument. I don't know that I'm ready to be his chum, but after several long talks with Esme, I can grudgingly appreciate the sacrifice he made skipping the sergeant's test to try and make it to our appointment. I want to have a forgiving heart. I do. But it's hard. Still, he's been so good about staying away, giving me space, I just wonder how he's truly adapting. I worry too much about him, I know.

Me<---idiot.

I'm sick to death of the animosity, which can't be good

for the kids. Still, I don't want to keep being so indecisive. Back and forth, back and forth. He does love the boys. Actually, he has a lot of good qualities; it's just the other stuff.

God, what will I do when he finds another woman?

Ugh. I feel sick.

Pilar arrived early at the school and gave in to the boys' pleas for a few minutes on the deserted playground. As long as they took care to stay clean, the chance to expend their bottle-pop energy would pay off in the long run. Better here than in front of their teachers, where she prayed they'd act like well-mannered little gentlemen.

She sat on a bench and watched them run from the slide to the swings, laughing and yelling to each other. As the evening breeze lifted her hair, Pilar closed her eyes and took advantage of the solitary time to gather her wits.

It had been a long week of anger and disillusionment since she had last seen Danny, and the thought of sitting next to him tonight absolutely frazzled her nerves. Despite it all, he'd had a magnetic pull on her psyche since girlhood. There was no sense trying to tell herself it'd be gone. That charming, solemn, devoted young man still existed somewhere deep inside the stranger she hardly knew anymore. Regrets burned in her throat. If only he hadn't shuttered himself from her in the first place. If only he had— just once—asked her what was wrong. If only he'd give her more than empty promises. . . .

Pilar sensed his presence as he approached from behind her, as though his very soul emitted sensory waves that her heart alone could detect. Her breath caught. *Will miracles never cease?* A blue flame of hope flickered inside her, softening her bitterness even further.

He came closer, and she stiffened, the hair at her nape prickling. She couldn't help but remember the living room kiss that had so shaken her resolve. Her breathing came fast and shallow when the breeze caught his woodsy aftershave and surrounded her with the memory-laden scent.

She kept her seat but hastily smoothed the skirt of her figure-hugging red chemise, an outfit she hadn't necessarily chosen knowing she'd see Danny. She just wanted to look nice for the meeting with the boys' teachers. But she knew it flattered her, especially with the five pounds she'd lost, and a small, fickle part of her hoped he'd notice.

All at once, the boys caught sight of Danny. Pilar could tell from the instantaneous brightening of their faces.

"Daddy!" they chimed in unison.

Like a high-velocity bullet, Teddy flew over the loose gravel in a flat-out sprint toward his father. His eyes were glued to Danny, so he couldn't possibly see the railroad tie edging around the swings, though it lay directly in his path.

Sucking in a sharp breath that smelled of wind and Danny and grilled dinner from a nearby house, Pilar lurched to her feet. She sensed the accident before it happened.

His left foot caught on the thick wood, ripping the shoe from it. Little Teddy sailed through the air and he hit the gravel chin first, his head slamming into the metal swingset frame with a sickening clang. His neck wrenched at an angle that made Pilar flinch, and his unnatural limpness and dead silence shot pain straight to her womb.

"Teddy!" she screamed, dropping her purse. Suddenly she was running, the spikes of her high heels gouging the gravel, her slim skirt yanking roughly against her thighs with each awkward stride. Her peripheral vision caught Pep running from another direction; she wanted to scream, "Stop!" before they had another collision, but horror strangled her silent.

Danny appeared at her side. He grabbed her elbow and steadied her the rest of the way. They fell to their knees next to Teddy, who still hadn't moved. Pilar's heart beat as though a demon dwelled inside it, determined to punch its way out. He was hurt. Really hurt.

"Oh . . . God. Baby!" She made ineffective jerky motions with her hands, starting to touch him, then stopping again. She knew she shouldn't shake him, but one primal part of her needed to rattle his cage. *Cry! Scream! Anything!*

"Teddy!" Danny shook him gently, then leaned his ear to the boy's back to listen. "Damn it, T, wake up." He felt for a pulse in Teddy's tiny neck. "Damn," Danny bit out, casting her a severe glance. "I have to start mouth-to-mouth—"

"H-he's not breathing?" She clutched at her throat, and the world swirled to a dark pinpoint that contained only this, only them. *Not her baby!*

Danny wrenched his leather jacket off. "Listen, run for help, Pilar. . . ."

Suddenly Teddy stirred, and they both froze. After one blood-gurgled inhale, his wail cut through the twilight like an off-tone siren. Pilar thought she'd never heard anything so wonderful in her life. She reached for Teddy with a violently trembling hand, touching him softly.

"We're here, Teddy." She brushed his brow.

Danny bent closer, running through the motions of rescue first aid again.

"D-daddy?"

"Lie still, Teddy boy, okay?"

"Mamaaaaa!" Teddy's tear-streaked face struggled to lift, and he flailed for her embrace.

"No, no, honey. Don't move!" *Madre de Dios!* So much blood. It covered the lower half of his face, filled his nose and mouth. Not only that, but a horrible purple goose egg had risen on his head.

Rigidity hit her like a lightning bolt, and she went dead still. Pep, who'd been hanging back, took one glance at his little brother's macabre state and threw himself into her arms, shaking and silent. Pilar rubbed his slight back as she peered down at her youngest son. "M-my God. Please, Danny—"

"Head wounds always bleed like hell," Danny assured her, his voice more relaxed than a glance at his face told Pilar he was. "Try to stay calm."

But Danny wasn't so together on the inside. Pilar could tell just looking at his ashen complexion. His focus completely on Teddy, Danny bent forward until his face was on the same level as his son's.

"Hey, little man." Teddy's cries nearly drowned out his words. "This'll be one to brag about at school, eh?" As he talked, he placed his leather jacket over Teddy's body.

"D-daddy!" Teddy gurgled. "M-my m-moooouth!"

"Your mouth looks good, big guy," Danny lied. "What else hurts, son?"

"My n-neck."

"Yeah? It looks good, too, T." As Danny spoke, he gently probed the skin at the back of Teddy's small neck. He flinched, and Danny placed a hand on his back. "You lie good and still, Teodoro. Do you hear me, guy?"

"D-don't l-leave me, Daddy!"

"I'm not going anywhere, T. Lie still." He glanced at Pilar. "Babe, run and—"

"Nooooo! Mama, don't goooo!" Teddy wailed.

Pilar crouched, the coppery wet smell of her little boy's blood registering horribly in her mind before numbness could block it. *Don't think about it.* She had to keep it together for Teddy. Pep still clung to her, but he wouldn't look at his little brother. "Mama's right here, sweet baby. I'm right here." She glanced beseechingly up at Danny. *Please don't make me leave my baby.*

"Damn it! There's no time . . ." Danny pressed a rough breath through his nose and fished in his pocket for his car keys. "Pep."

Pep turned toward his father, teeth chattering.

Danny smiled encouragingly, though Pilar could see the urgency in his cocoa-brown eyes. "Can you be my partner here, buddy?" Danny asked their son.

"Y-yes." Pep swallowed audibly.

Danny lobbed him the keys. "Run to Daddy's car—"

"Not through the parking lot, Danny." Pilar's voice was reedy and high-pitched. "He's too upset."

Danny rubbed his free hand up and down her back in long, soothing strokes, but his eyes stayed on Pep. "I parked just on the edge of the playground, babe. He won't even have to go into the lot. We need an ambulance."

"Of course, you're right." She whipped a glance around the schoolyard, but found it empty other than them. Where was everyone when they needed them?

"Pep, unlock the car and get my cell phone, son. Can you do that?"

"I-in the glove compartment?"

"Yes." He spoke in well-modulated tones, his eyes boring directly into his son's. "You remember how to dial nine-one-one?"

"Uh-huh. And, press send, right?" Pep tugged at his collar.

"You got it, buddy. Press send and speak nice and clear, do you hear me? Take a good, deep breath."

Pilar dragged in her own lungful of fear-tanged air as she watched Pep's skinny little chest expand and contract.

"Tell them you're my son, and that your brother is badly hurt. Good and calm. My name is Officer . . . ?"

"Daniel Valenzuela," Pep obediently answered.

"From district . . . ?"

"Four."

"Good man." Danny clapped a hand on his shoulder and squeezed. "Ask them to send an ambulance to the school, and keep them on the line. Talk to them while you're walking back, okay? So I can talk to them after you. Got all that?"

Pep seemed to absorb calmness and confidence from his father's apparent faith in his abilities. He stood straighter, face flushed. "Yeah, daddy. I can do it."

"I know you can, *mi hijo*. Now, go on."

Pep hesitated, sliding a reluctant sidelong glance toward the growing pool of blood around Teddy's chin.

"Hey." Danny whistled sharply to redirect his attention. When Pep looked at him, Danny winked, the waning sunset glowing rosy-gold off the smile lines around his eyes. His words, however, were firm and compelling. "Your brother will be fine, *mi hijo*. I promise. I need you to make that call."

Pep whipped a confirming glance at Pilar, and she managed a shaky smile. "Listen to your daddy, sweetheart. Go on. Watch where you're running!"

A boy with an important job, Pep took off like the wind. Pilar's eyes jerked to Teddy, who'd grown way too quiet. "His h-head, Danny. Look at the—"

"Pilar." Danny lay a finger across his lips, then pointed to Teddy. "He'll be fine. But . . ." He shook his head.

She understood. Danny didn't want Teddy to realize how badly he was hurt, or shock might become a real problem. Instead of talking about Teddy, Pilar wiggled down onto her stomach facing him and spoke in soft, motherly reassurances. He'd lost teeth, and as Pilar collected them from the bloody gravel, she silently hoped they were baby teeth—as if there weren't more serious issues to worry about.

It seemed like forever, but in reality was mere moments before Pep returned, the phone to his ear. A young woman Pilar recognized as the attendance secretary trotted alongside him, and she stopped to collect the spilled contents of Pilar's purse.

As Pep came into hearing range, Pilar heard him saying, "He's right here. Hold on." He closed the distance between them in a run, holding the phone out. "They wanna talk to you, Daddy!"

Danny sat back on his haunches and took the phone from Pep, pulling the boy against his chest as he spoke in official-sounding phrases. *Loss of consciousness. Possible neck or head injury. Definite shock. Deep laceration.*

Approaching sirens tore the deafening silence of the evening, and relief rushed through Pilar. Time seemed so slow and distorted; she thought they'd never get there.

Pep, looking stronger for having done a man's job, leaned toward his little brother. "You have a really awesome bump on your head, but you're gonna be okay, Teddy Bed-wetty."

"That's not my name," Teddy murmured, in a tone utterly devoid of the vehemence with which he usually defended himself against the hated nickname.

Pep seemed to notice, growing very earnest. "Till you get better, I'll do all your chores, 'kay? And, next time we're at Unca'vino's, you can sit in the driver's seat first."

"Swear?" Teddy mumbled listlessly.

Pep drew an X over his chest, eyes round and solemn. "Hope to die, stick a needle in my eye."

"'Kay." Teddy took a rattly breath.

Pilar's throat closed with emotion and her gaze drifted to Danny's just as he snapped the phone closed. They had such good boys, and their shared glance acknowledged that. He offered his hand, and she gladly took it. Nothing mattered right now except Teddy.

The ambulance arrived, throwing blue and red lights against the trees, and disgorged the paramedics in a mad rush of glare and equipment and sound. Pilar literally had to drag herself away from Teddy's side, but Danny was right. They needed room to work. Their clipped phrases rang like dialogue from an episode of ER; she couldn't bear to think of it in relation to her little boy.

Get a pressure bandage on that laceration.

Watch the C-spine.

Pep remained unusually quiet, sitting cross-legged on the grass next to her feet. Danny pulled her back against his warm, solid chest, and she didn't resist. On the contrary, she felt tearfully grateful for the comfort and his warmth as he cradled her emotionally as well as physically.

Patient's immobilized.

Start an IV.

I can't get a vein. He's too small.

She shuddered, and Danny smoothed his palms over the goose bumps on her forearms. It felt good, she acknowledged, as she watched the EMTs work on her son.

"You know them?" She asked Danny without turning.

His murmured "mm-hmm" rumbled through his chest into her back. "They're a good crew. Don't worry."

They had braced Teddy's neck and strapped a backboard to him, securing his head to it. Pilar sucked in a breath and held it as they prepared to move him.

The slim paramedic in charge said, "Okay, slowly. On my count. One, two, three."

Pilar winced as they flipped him over, but sagged with relief when she saw Teddy's eyes were open. Danny's warm, muscled arms tightened around her, as though he could fortify her courage with his physical strength. She felt his lips against her hair whispering, "Easy. He's doing good," but her heart in her throat silenced any response.

By this time, the light show had drawn a crowd. Word was sent to Pep and Teddy's teachers, and the young secretary had taken care to brush off and return Pilar's purse.

After they'd secured Teddy on a gurney, Pilar, Danny, and Pep walked alongside as the paramedics steered him toward the ambulance. It became a jumble of motion and outstretched arms, murmured reassurances and brief touches. Soon the head paramedic, a birdlike giant with wise green eyes, turned toward them. Removing his surgical gloves, he ran a huge hand through his wiry nest of blond hair. "You wanna ride, V?"

"No, Jason. He needs his mother more than me."

That's not true! He needs us both, Pilar wanted to cry out. But, they couldn't both ride with Teddy, and already Danny's warm hand was urging her forward into the yawning glare of the ambulance interior. He braced her elbow as she stepped up clumsily. She shivered, and Danny handed her his leather jacket, then glanced toward Jason, pulling Pep against his side. "We'll follow you."

Jason shut one of the rear ambulance doors, but as he reached for the other, Danny grabbed the edge of it.

"Punky."

She turned.

He winked, as if to reassure. Just like he'd done when Pep had been frightened. "I'm right behind you, P."

She nodded, pulling the lapels of his jacket around her neck. The leather released a scent that was pure Danny—woodsy and masculine with just a touch of the vinyl polish he religiously used on the Chevelle's interior. The familiarity soothed her then like Danny's calmness had in the midst of the ordeal. What would she have done had he not been there? Handled it, obviously. She wasn't helpless.

Still, his reassurances, his mere presence, had kept her sane in the first moments when she'd seen Teddy, pale and limp, all that blood. She shuddered, sinking into the jacket.

She sat next to Teddy as the ambulance rolled, the memories replaying in her mind like film clips. Danny, chin to injured chin with his son. The crinkles around his eyes when he winked at Pep. The breadth and heat of his chest, the comfort of his nearness, and his lips against her hair.

The thoughts imbued her with the strength to be courageous for Teddy and not to think of anything else—like the future. Lord have mercy, she did not want to raise these sons on her own. The realization hit her like a siren's wail. The boys did need their father, despite what Danny had said. She hated to admit it, but she needed him, too.

The first hour in the hospital was a blur. Teddy had been unconscious for no more than two minutes, but that was long enough to warrant a battery of extra tests. An X-ray machine had been rolled into the room, and Teddy was scheduled for a CAT scan. After that came a body exam, more X rays, lab work, stitches, and cleanup. Several hours elapsed before Teddy was finished, before Pilar was convinced he'd be okay.

Much to everyone's relief, the injuries turned out to be less serious than they'd feared, though Teddy wouldn't be running through playgrounds anytime soon. He'd lost five teeth—all babies—and the gash on his chin required three stitches. His neck was stiff, and two black eyes gave him the look of a baby panda bear. The impact had bruised his chest, and his head against the swingset left him with a sizable goose egg and a concussion. If that weren't enough, his palms and forearms were covered with oozy gravel burn, and his very favorite Broncos jersey had been cut off and discarded.

He was one bummed-out little guy, but at least he was going home, just as soon as the doctor returned with discharge instructions. Pilar could hardly wait. Her fear, coupled with the odor of disinfectant and the sound of Teddy's cries, had left her with a pounding headache. She could only imagine how poor Teddy felt.

Danny, who'd been at the nurses' station calling family and friends, moved silently into the curtained area where Pilar had been sitting with the boys. She looked up and his face warmed, which made her immediately look away. Her heart pounded and her palms grew moist.

Already, she'd begun to second-guess her emotions from the ambulance. Yes, she'd been frightened. Yes, she appreciated Danny's support. But now that the worst was over, the truth of their situation rushed back to suck her under, like an unexpected riptide. She had been so needy, so accepting of Danny's comfort. Fear for Teddy—that's all it was. Right?

As though the last three weeks had never occurred, Danny slipped his hand beneath her hair to cup and massage her neck, exactly the way she liked it. He leaned in. "You okay, Punkybean?" he asked, his mouth so close she felt the caress of his breath on her cheek.

"Ah . . . yeah, I'm uh . . ." She pulled away as subtly as she could. She didn't want the boys to read into the familiarity and harbor false hope, but she didn't want to seem angry, either. Though Pep appeared occupied with toys a nurse had given him, Pilar had no doubt he was attuned to every nuance of his parents' interactions. He still couldn't understand why Daddy was staying at Uncle Ruben's. More than anything, Pep just wanted them to be a family again.

"Pilar?" Danny whispered.

She crossed to the foot of the bed, then turned back to him. Determined not to let her flip-flopped emotions make promises she wasn't sure she could keep, she tossed her hair and lifted her chin. "I'll be fine as soon as I can take Teddy home."

I . . . not we.

"Of course," Danny murmured, but his eyes said, *So that's how it's gonna be.* Whatever bonding they'd gained at the school had been temporary, he clearly realized, and he looked crushed. He laid his palm on Teddy's shoulder, studying his tiny sleeping form. Danny's chin tremored, and his nostrils flared sharply. "Thank God he's going to be okay. Poor guy. Scared me half to death."

The show of emotion made her breath catch. God, she felt heartless. She'd greedily taken all the comfort he'd offered during the ordeal, but the moment things settled down, she repaid him with a solid snub. Impending divorce aside, that wasn't the kind of person she wanted to be.

She tried to make amends for acting so selfishly with a softened tone. "How are you doing?"

"How am I?" he asked, clearly still fixed on her brush-off. His eyes narrowed, and he pursed his lips. "Not good, P. Not good at all, if you really want to know."

I meant, with this, she wanted to add. *With Teddy.* "Well"—a tight swallow—"you were wonderful."

"Apparently not wonderful enough."

She sighed. They were talking in riddles and subtext, but she couldn't find the right words to make it stop. Her hand snaked around the cold metal bar at the end of Teddy's bed for support.

"We'll both have different perspectives in the morning. Things'll look better then." Her gaze slid to her son.

"You think?" His voice grew husky. "Because tomorrow, and the day after, the next year, the rest of my life, Pilar, they look nothing but bleak to me."

"I was talking about Teddy."

"Yeah? Well, I think we need to talk about us."

"Not here." Her throat ached with unreleased emotion. She blinked several times. "Please."

"Then where? When? I may still be in your private purgatory for my unforgivable sins, but I know we can work through it. I'm not willing to give up." His left hand slid along the bed's sidebar as he approached her, his wedding band zinging like a long musical note against the metal.

She stared down at the band Danny hadn't yet removed, the band he hadn't removed, as a matter of fact, for the fourteen years since she'd placed it on his finger. Self-consciously, she curled her bare left hand into her body, riddled with guilt. She hadn't wanted to take hers off yet, but a TV divorce therapist had suggested doing so as a symbolic first step to moving on. So angry after the missed mediation appointment, she'd just reacted. She looked at Danny's well-worn band, talons of regret gouging her heart. Clearly he wasn't moving anywhere, and part of her was terrified to leave him behind.

"That's right," he said, and her gaze snapped to his face. "I'm still married. *I'm* still wearing it. I guess I don't have as quick of an on-and-off switch as you."

"I don't want to talk about it." She wondered if the words were as honest as they'd once been.

"How can you say that?" Cords of muscle stood out along his neck, spanning out toward his wide shoulders. "Our marriage is the most important thing in my life."

"I meant, about the divor—" She sighed and pressed two trembling fingers against her forehead, closing her eyes. He knew what she meant, and she wouldn't be baited in front of the boys. She peered over at Pep again, and Danny cupped her elbow and pulled her outside the curtains.

"He can't hear us now. No excuses."

Bitter heat ripped through her. "You know what I'm saying. The divorce won't just disappear because of what happened tonight. Nothing's solved. You aren't being fair—"

"Fair?" An emotion both cold and hot flashed in his eyes. He jerked his chin to the side in a restrained shrug. "Forgive me, but you know what they say about all being fair in love and war."

War? Teeth clenched, she leaned in. "That's what this is now? War?"

"Absolutely not," he enunciated. "God, I feel like I'm banging my head against a brick wall. This is love, Pilar Valenzuela, though maybe the dark side. We've sure as hell seen better times, but, this"—he placed one palm over his heart, the other over hers—"you and me, this is *love*. For better or for worse. Remember those words?"

How dare he throw wedding vows in her face! She stepped back from his touch. "What about cherish?" she snapped. "Did you forget that one?" Spinning away, she reached up and caressed her temples, trying to quash the burst of bitterness. Long moments passed, during which Pilar felt every hot pulse of blood through her veins.

"Did I, Punky?" came Danny's emotionally shredded reply.

She turned back.

He looked crestfallen. "Because if my actions didn't show how much I cherished you, I swear, I didn't intend—" he cut himself off and fought for the right words. "I never knew you felt that way."

She hadn't expected that, and for a moment, didn't know what to say. How could he not have known? The silences and forgotten events. The disappointments, the distance. Working all the time. How could she have been the only one to see it?

She reached up and wound her fingers in the chain of the diamond pendant he had bought her when Pep was born. *Tell him,* her mind whispered. *Now or never.*

"Yeah, you did forget. You forgot the word, the vow, and you forgot *me*. That's what I can't live with."

"I never meant to forget you." His eyes flashed with sincerity. "If it didn't show, give me a chance to change."

"Oh, yet another chance?" She scoffed.

"And another, and another, until I fumble through and get it right, *yes*. Just like I'd do for you. Aren't we worth it?" He waited, but she didn't answer. "I was showing you love the only way I knew how, P. I didn't know I was failing you." He clasped his hands. "Can't you see that?"

She tried to shake the confusion from her mind. "I d-don't know. Didn't the distance bother you, too, or are you able to survive in an emotional vacuum?"

The skin tightened across his prominent cheekbones. Pain-shadowed eyes searched her face. "Maybe I'm less emotionally insightful than you, but I never intentionally forgot you or our sons. Every day I get up and go to work, every overtime minute I spend away is for you and our boys. It's how I show my love, being the kind of husband and father I never had. I thought you knew that much about me."

She squeezed her eyes shut, blocking out the rush of tenderness. Damn it, she had known that, somewhere along the line. Was she wrong about the divorce? If so, why did she hurt so much? "Please don't say any more. I don't want to fight. It's been a rough night—" Her words caught, and she covered her mouth with her hand. She couldn't bear his remorse now, on top of her confusion. She felt a light hand on her forehead, his palm smoothing down her cheek.

"It's been rough—for all of us. But we hung together, like always." He placed a soft kiss on her hairline. "I'll do anything to make things better, Punky, except divorce you without a fight. When I told my mother about the separation, do you know what she said?"

Pilar's heart took a sickening plunge. "What?"

"She said, Don't lose the best thing life ever gave you, *mi hijo*. Ruben's better off without that Merrilee, but Pilar is a gem. Go get your family back, whatever it takes." He paused, searching her face. When he spoke again, his voice was hoarse. "Mother knows best. You've got to forgive me for the damned appointment. Give me a chance."

"Fine, if that's what you want to hear." She waved his plea away, trying not to focus on Rosario's heartbreakingly sweet words. "But you don't seem to understand—if you hurt me again, I'll shatter. I can't take the risk."

His hand snaked around her wrist, and he lifted her fingers to his lips. "I won't hurt you"—a kiss on her palm—"if you help me to realize when I'm doing something stupid. Don't grin and bear it; be honest with me. Help me."

"I . . ." She sighed. "Danny . . ."

He released her hand, but pulled her into an embrace that was more desperate than tender. She couldn't make herself move away. His hand cupped the back of her head, smoothed her hair, his heartbeat strong and steady against her. "I know we can work, Pilar. Say you know it, too."

"I-I don't know." She stiffened in his hold, but her words had no oomph. "Please. I can't deal with this now, on top of everything else." His arms slackened, and she extracted herself. Stepping away, she shored up her dignity, smoothing her grass-stained dress. "Let's think about Teddy."

His eyes shone unusually bright in his haggard

face. But his voice—that was the worst. Forlorn and imploring. "I *am* thinking about him. And his brother, and how much they need their parents—"

"Daddy?" Teddy croaked, his voice no more than a dry whisper from the other side of the curtain. After a split-second pause during which he studied her face, Danny brushed aside the curtain to go to his son.

Pilar remained outside and willed her adrenaline to dissipate. As the sounds of their soft murmurs reached her ears, she backed against the wall and slumped, closing her eyes. Her resistance to him was slipping away.

Dare she believe an apology—another empty promise perhaps—might have the strength to correct the massive structural damage to their marriage? *But he'd said so much more than that.*

A seedling of doubt took root in her heart, and she bit her lip. Suppose he truly hadn't known how unhappy she'd been? As her disillusionment had mounted, things had just grown quieter and quieter in their home until the silence became painful and deafening. Until she couldn't bear to hear *nothing* anymore.

A shudder ran through her, and she wrapped her arms around her torso to stave off the soul-deep cold. Realizing she still wore Danny's soft jacket, redolent with his scent and softly shaped to his body, she slipped her thumbs up under the lapels. She lifted the leather to her face and indulged in one more long breath of him before she reluctantly shrugged it off to give it back. That scent, she knew, would chase her to her grave. Feeling choking indecision like a tightly bound gag in her mouth, she pushed aside the curtain and joined her bedraggled family.

Danny's head came up as she neared. "Teddy wants to know if I'll be staying with him tonight." His searching eyes said so much more than the words that formed the simple statement.

Oh, God. She didn't know if she could resist his comfort if they slept beneath the same roof. She opened her mouth to protest when Teddy's rough little plea stopped her.

"Please, Mama."

Her heart wrenched. Teddy needed his daddy. She peered at Danny again, chewing the inside of her cheek. It shocked her to realize how much she wanted him there. For Teddy. Now wasn't the time to worry about anything other than her injured little boy. She placed her hand gently on Teddy's tummy and smiled. "Of course, Teddy bear. We'll all be there together—me, you, Daddy, and Pep."

Six

Addendum to Pilar Valenzuela's journal entry, Monday, September 24:

The house is dark except for the glow of Teddy's night-light next to me here on the floor. I can't sleep. Danny and I are taking turns looking in on Teddy, but I figured as long as I was lying there staring at the ceiling, I might as well come listen to my baby's breathing.

Thank God Teddy's safe. Still, the trial isn't over. A second concussion within the next couple weeks could be very serious, the doctor said. It will be a full-time job keeping Teddy inactive that long.

Danny's here. Two rooms over.

It should be normal, but it's not.

What could I say to an injured little boy's pleas for his father? No? To tell the truth, it's a relief to share this fear, this responsibility for keeping Teddy safe. We have to wake him every two hours and ask him a bunch of questions just to make sure he's coherent. I'm terrified that the next time I go to wake him, it won't work, or I'll sleep through my alarm, or that I'll lose the battle against my weakness and return to the guest-room bed with Danny, just to feel his warmth surround me. God.

Me<---wimp.

I can't sleep for wanting to feel him. Having Danny home, but in another room, is awful. I miss him. I'll admit it. So damn much that sometimes I feel like I can't breathe. I still don't know if we can work things out, but what if, for the boys' sake, we start by being friends? Isn't that how we started in the first place? Oops, someone's coming.

Pilar managed to scramble to her feet just as the door began to squeak on its hinges. Expecting Danny, she held her breath and her journal equally tight as the golden cone of light spilled into the dark room. But it was Pep, not Danny, who shadowed the doorway. His belly stuck out and he rubbed one eye with the back of his hand, like he'd done since he was a toddler.

"Mama?" he croaked.

She set the notebook aside and went to him, pulling him against her. "Shh, what's the matter, honey?"

"I had a bad dream 'bout Teddy." He flickered a worried glance at his brother's twin bed. "Is he okay?"

"Sure, beetle bug." She smiled to reassure him, then urged him into the room. "Want to come see?"

Pep nodded. They crept to Teddy's bedside and Pep peered over, holding his breath until his battered little brother blew out a quivery-lipped exhale. A mischievous smile brightened Pep's face, and he scrunched his shoulders and peered up at Pilar. She tilted her head toward the door. They tiptoed out of the room and into Pep's.

When she had him all tucked in, she sat on his

bed and rubbed his chest, loving him so much it took her a moment to speak. She didn't want him to hold his emotions in. Reaching out, she smoothed his pajama top, then she stretched out beside him, propping herself up on one elbow. Pep nestled against her. "Want a story?"

"Naw. Just stay here for a little bit."

"Okay." She indulged in the pleasure of cradling her son, considering he was at the age where he didn't allow it all the time. When Pep's body had relaxed, she cleared her throat. "That was pretty scary tonight, huh?"

"Yeah. Lotsa blood."

"Now you know why I'm always nagging you yard monkeys not to run." She tickled him, and he squirmed and giggled. A moment later he was silent again. "What are you thinking about, Pep?"

"Stuff."

"What stuff, *mi hijo*?"

Round, solemn eyes rose to implore hers. "Does Daddy get to come home now? He said he was sorry, and you always say it's not good to hold a crutch."

She swallowed thickly. "Grudge."

"Yeah, a grudge."

Her stomach contracted. *Damn.* Pep had heard them arguing at the hospital. She sighed. "It's not as simple as that . . . but I don't want you to worry about—"

"But why not?" His voice wobbled, and his eyes filled with moisture. "We're a family, and he 'pologized. It should be simple. He's my daddy. I don't wanna divorce him."

"Oh, sweetheart, you won't div—" She sighed, feeling sick over Pep's anguish and hopelessly inept at easing it. "Listen. He'll always be your Daddy. No matter what."

"I miss him every day, Mama. I love him."

"I—" *Love him, too,* she was about to say. She bit her lip, hating that Pep was troubled. "I know you do, Pep. He loves you, too. And so do I."

"Do you love Daddy?"

She looked away, plucking at a yarn tie on Pep's quilt. Her eldest son always cut to the chase. He wanted to know *what* he wanted to know, *when* he wanted to know it. Period. Such her little man.

"Do you, Mama?"

He'd know if she lied. "Of course I do, bug."

Pep flapped his arms. "So why don't you just tell him, so we can be a family again? In this house, like always."

Sadness took hold at his simplistic view of things. She kissed his forehead. "This is between me and your father. I don't want you to worry—" She tapped his nose "—okay? No matter what, we're still your mama and daddy, and we love you to pieces. Now go to sleep."

"Okay," he said grudgingly.

She waited until he'd snuggled down, then rose and walked to the door, switching off his light. Her eyes adjusted to the dim orange glow from his race-car night-light.

As she was closing the door, Pep stopped her. "Mama?"

"Yes?" For a moment she wondered if she imagined he'd called her. When he finally spoke, she could barely hear him.

"*I* cherish you," he whispered. "Can that be enough so Daddy can come home? Please?"

Awed and humbled, she leaned her cheek against the edge of the door and stared through the darkness at the wonderful little soul she was so lucky to have as a son. She carefully sidestepped his question. "Honey. I cherish you, too."

In the moments before wakefulness took hold, Danny imagined the divorce had been a bad dream. He heard Pilar's gentle words, smelled her spicy-sweet skin, and figured she was waking him to make love, like she used to do. God, he loved her body. Even more so since childbirth had left a few marks, like beautiful badges of honor. They only served to make her more womanly to him, softer and more enticing. *His.*

Eyes closed in decadent drowsiness, he rolled toward the sound of her voice and reached out, thrilled when his palm made contact with her lush, round breast. He heard her gasp, and a smile curved his lips. One of the best things about Pilar was her lack of vocal inhibition. He never had to wonder what she wanted or liked—she made it abundantly clear.

He kneaded her soft flesh, the moan low and rough in his throat. Her nipple pebbled against his hand, and his body reacted. "I want to be inside you, baby girl." He pulled her closer. "Let me feel you—"

Something like a handcuff clamped his wrist, stopping the wicked caress. "Danny!" came Pilar's voice. Stern.

He frowned and squinted, just in time to see Pilar shove his hand away. His eyes snapped open fully, then, as she backed toward the door.

Lurching up so quickly it brought stars to his vision, he raked his fingers through his hair and fought for his bearings. The guest room. Reality struck like a hollow-point bullet. Oh, yeah. "Pilar. I-I'm sorry. I was dreaming."

A flare of . . . awareness sapped the shuttered look from her eyes. Making no move to leave, no move to come closer, she crossed her arms over her chest and moistened her lips with a nervous flick of her tongue. "It's your turn."

God, he slept too heavy. Must have something to do with being home, in a bed that didn't feel like a medieval torture device, between sheets that smelled like . . . Pilar's fabric softener. Damn.

Teddy! Immediately sobered, he yanked off the covers and swung his feet to the floor, reaching up to rub his eyes. "Shoot. Did I oversleep?"

"No. . . ." She started forward, then stopped. The telltale wash of color rose up her neck and her gaze fluttered away. She felt the wanting, too. He could see it all over her like a full-body tattoo. For now, he'd leave it alone. *For now.*

With a deep breath, she raised her eyes. "He's fine. I woke him half an hour ago. But . . . I thought I'd try and get some sleep. . . ."

"Okay. You go on." He crossed to the chair in the corner to retrieve the T-shirt he'd shed earlier. He wouldn't normally cover his bare chest, but things were different. Pilar wouldn't want him half-dressed. As he pulled the wear-softened cotton over his head, he tried to wash the night-blurred images of her, the feel of her body, from his mind.

"You want me to make you some coffee?"

Always so thoughtful, his Pilar. Even now. "You don't have to wait on me. Go on to bed."

He would've thought she'd take advantage of the opportunity to flee, but instead she leaned against the doorjamb, feet crossed. His gaze dropped to those damn ridiculous cow slippers she so dearly loved, and he bit the inside corner of his mouth to keep from smiling. "Something on your mind?"

"Pep heard us."

He frowned. "Come again?"

"At the hospital. Pep heard us talking." She swept her hair into an impromptu ponytail and held it. He tried not to notice the little curls that escaped to dance against her neck. "He said, 'I cherish you, Mama. Can that be enough so Daddy can come home?' " She paused. "I don't want him thinking he can control things, Danny. It's too big a burden for a little boy." She released a small growl. "I'd hoped this separation wouldn't affect them."

Even as he tried to repress it, he could feel gaping disbelief on his face. "You're kidding, right?"

"No." She gave a few fluttery blinks and her chin jutted stubbornly. "Our marriage is between us, not them."

"They're our sons. Take it from me, children become an unwitting part of any marital problems."

He moved closer, drawn by the softness of her skin. Unable to resist, he reached out and ran the backs of his fingers down the silk of her cheek. She didn't pull back, but he saw her neck move with a tight swallow. "There's nothing we can do about it if you insist on divorce."

"You're just trying to make me feel guilty."

"No, I'm being realistic." He tried to lighten his tone, because the sight of her in the doorway, forlorn and torn and chewing her lip, sprang a well of compassion inside him. "If you get the divorce, you'll live here, I'll live somewhere else. It's called a *broken* home." He let that sink in. "You understand that, right?"

"Yeah, but we can make sure it doesn't . . . affect them," she offered, none too sure of herself.

God, he wanted to hold her. Or shake her. "Punky, darlin' . . ." Hands on his hips, he hung his head and expelled a breath. His words would hurt her, and he hated that. More than anything, he wanted to make things up to her. Why did it seem so impossible at every turn? "It will affect them. I'm not saying it'll destroy them, but joint custody, splitting their time between two houses, will affect them. It's a fact." He toyed with the wisdom of going on. She needed to hear it. "If you break up our family, that's a by-product you'll have to accept."

A maelstrom of emotions crossed her face. Guilt, indecision, anger, and futility. Finally she slid down to the ground. "Damn it, why does this have to be so difficult?"

Pilar wasn't a weeper, yet he could tell she was past

due for a good cry. But he knew her well enough to realize she'd die before letting him see what she'd perceive as weakness. *Her mother's daughter.*

Danny shook his head, filled with a tangle of frustration and tenderness. If only she'd express her dissatisfaction instead of letting it fester. She needed to learn that he didn't expect her to smile prettily and endure life. But he also wanted her to realize she didn't have to end things cold turkey to find happiness, and if she did, there would be repercussions. "Because it is difficult, Punky. It's a life-changing decision for all of us."

Pilar's stoic silence tore at his heart. Part of him wanted to hug her. Another wanted to force her to see how wrong this was for all of them, but instead he grudgingly told her what *she* needed to hear. Just this once.

"Look, it's going to be okay." He nudged her arm until she lifted her dry, drawn face, then offered his hand. She took it, and he pulled her straight up into a hug, rocking her side to side. "We'll figure it out for the boys, Pilar. I won't lie—you'll never convince me divorce is for the best—"

"I don't want to ar—"

"Shh." He pressed his fingers gently against her lips. "I'm not trying to argue. Hear me out."

Her body stiffened.

"From now on, we'll work out what we can for the boys. That's all I'm saying. Okay? I don't want them hurt, either."

Her hackles lowered. "But they will be."

A beat passed. "I'd say, they probably already are."

The shuddering sigh she expelled seemed to deplete her of energy. "I'm a terrible, selfish mother."

"Don't be ridiculous. The boys worship you. Now, come on. You're exhausted." He tucked her under his arm and steered her to the hallway. "It's been one hell of a day. You need some rest."

She shuffled next to him, defeated. Their cadence was off, and she jostled under his arm with every step as though they were sluggish participants in a three-legged race. His lips twisted ruefully. How symbolic. Walking next to each other through life, yet hearing different drummers. But, were they, really? Or did one of them just have two left feet?

When he'd settled her into her bed—their bed—he backed off. There'd be time for discussion when she wasn't exhausted almost to the point of incoherence.

They murmured good nights and he turned to leave, but he stopped in the doorway. What had Sgt. Obermeyer said about women needing more than what he'd always given Pilar? He turned and stared through the semidarkness at her tiny form. "How about I bring you some of that tea you like? It'll relax you. Help you sleep."

Her liquid brown eyes warmed, cautiously, hopefully. "If you don't mind. That'd be nice." She pulled the comforter up around her chest and pressed it down with her arms, looking almost embarrassed by his offer. "Thanks."

His smile came slowly. "My pleasure."

Ten minutes later, he carried the steaming tea back down the hall and paused to check the boys before taking it in to Pilar. He peeked in on Pep first—

sleeping soundly. Next stop, Teddy's room. Dan set the cup on the bureau and crossed over, angling his head as he peered down on his black-and-blue son. He placed his palm on Teddy's scraped-up tummy.

Teddy stirred, then opened his eyes. "Daddy . . ."

"Hey, little man." Dan tucked the quilt his mother had made for Teddy when he was a baby. "How you feeling?"

Teddy's eyelids drooped, and he made little chewing motions before murmuring, "Head hurts."

I'll bet. "You know why?"

He shifted beneath the patchwork, settling into a tight fetal position, his back to Danny. "I fell at the school," came his sleep-slurred answer. "'Cuz I was runnin' and mama says not to run."

Danny smiled. "It's okay to run, *hijito,* if you watch where you're going."

"And those doctors cut my Broncos jersey."

A soft laugh lifted Danny's shoulders, and love filled his chest. "We'll get you a new jersey, don't worry. Go to sleep, buddy." But the suggestion was unnecessary. Teddy was out cold.

As Danny turned to retrieve the teacup, the nightlight-illuminated cover of Pilar's journal grabbed his attention. *Read me,* it whispered seductively. He stood at-gunpoint still, heart pounding with warning. What in the hell? He'd never invaded her privacy. She had hundreds of journals stored somewhere in this house, and he'd never so much as cracked a single binding. But there it was. Beckoning. If he could just get into her head a little bit, get some kind of handle on where he stood. . . .

No. It wasn't right. He threw a guilty glance over his shoulder and tunneled his fingers restlessly through his hair. Did he dare?

The journal drew him again. He tugged at the bottom of his T-shirt and crossed his arms. Then uncrossed them. Busy movement—ridiculous. His fists clenched and unclenched as he moved toward the journal like he was stalking it. Squatting, he lifted the sleek red notebook and smoothed his palm over the cover. This was one of those no-turning-back moments, like committing a crime. Once you'd crossed the line, that was it. Period. His seventeen-year record of never having invaded her privacy would be forever lost.

Worth the risk? He fanned the page edges thoughtfully . . . considering. Hadn't he said all was fair in love and war? If the key to winning her back was inked on the pages of this book and he didn't look, he'd never forgive himself. Ruben told him to do whatever it took. All's fair. Desperate times called for desperate measures. What other clichés could he apply to rationalize his actions?

A jolt of nerves lifted his eyes to the door once, then he released a tense breath and opened the book. He wanted his wife back. He didn't know where else to look for answers, and Pilar certainly wasn't offering any. *What did he have to lose?*

Danny crept silently into the master bedroom. Pilar's back was turned to him, the profile of her body an inviting, womanly undulation beneath the comforter. For a moment he thought she might have drifted off. But when he set the teacup on the nightstand, her movement rustled the sheets and her eyes found his.

Her skin looked velvety in the golden lamp glow. Wavy auburn hair spilled over the pillow and her eyelids drooped drowsily. The down comforter had tugged her silk nightgown tightly against her breasts, and he couldn't make himself look away. Such aching beauty. The mother of his sons.

He feared he couldn't speak, but then she scooted up and sat against the brass headboard pipes, breaking the spell.

He gestured toward the cup. "Your tea, milady."

"You found the tea bags and everything. Wow." She tucked her hair behind those ears he loved to nibble and reached for the cup, blowing steam off the front as she held it. Her round, wary eyes tracked his movements. In between blowing, she cleared the sleepiness from her throat. "What took you so long?"

"I checked the boys." He sat on the end of the bed, smiling in a way he hoped would convey his unspoken secret—being friends was a good place to start. His heart soared, remembering the words of confusion and desire she'd written. Deep inside, she wanted him to find his way back inside her heart . . . and he would.

"Everything okay?" She still hadn't sipped the tea.

"Yeah. Pep's out cold and Teddy woke up to talk to me."

"Good. What did he say?"

"He said he got hurt at school because he was running, and *'Mama says not to run.'*"

She laughed. "At least some of my nagging is sinking in. That's a good sign." As though their easy camaraderie had taken her by surprise, she blinked and let her gaze flutter down into the cup.

"I added one sugar cube and a big squirt of lemon juice."

One eyebrow arched, and she took a sip. "Mmm. Thanks. I didn't know you knew how I liked it."

He moved farther up and sat cross-legged beside her, trying his best to read her body language. He didn't want to push. "I knew. But I should've taken advantage of that knowledge more often." He paused. "I'm sorry."

A tension-wrought chasm of the unsaid stretched between them. Their eyes locked. Danny couldn't tear himself away from her. God help him, he didn't want to leave. The moment took on a surreal quality that entranced him, as though death had stolen his love, and this was but her filmy ghost come to pay him one last visit. He had so much to say, so much regret. He feared if he looked away, she would disappear, and where would he be then? "Pilar . . ."

She said nothing at first, but he watched her, unable to take a full breath. As she twisted to set the cup on the saucer, he admired the expanse of smooth caramel skin that showed above the deep vee back of her gown, desperately wanting to touch it.

She faced him again. "Danny?"

"Yes?"

Her hands smoothed the comforter covering her lap in a wide arc. "C-can you do something for me," she whispered, "without reading too much into it? Three things, actually." She nibbled the corner of her mouth, looking uncertain.

His heart leapt. "Anything, baby girl."

"I want to hold off on mediation for a while. All this with Teddy . . . it just isn't practical."

Stunned, he almost forgot to answer. "Whatever you say. What else?"

"Will you"—she blinked worriedly—"stay for the week and help me with Teddy?"

"You don't even have to ask." His heart began to drum. "Request number three?"

Looking dubious and needy, she dragged back the covers, exposing her legs, bare beneath the hem of her gown. "Will you hold me?" Her voice faltered. "Just for tonight?"

Not just for tonight, love. Forever. He wanted to say it, but he didn't, determined to let her take the lead in this blindman's bluff game of finding their way back to each other. He crawled up the bedcovers, his motions languid. "I'll hold you as much as you want me to, Punky."

He slid between the sheets and molded his body to the back of hers, tucking her head on his shoulder. Her hair smelled like home and heaven, and her skin slipped against his like an elusive memory. He combed the tumbled curls back from her forehead and kissed her there, on her ear, and on the side of her neck. "Sleep, P. Teddy's okay, and I'm here. Everything will be fine, I promise."

A sigh shuddered from her as the tension left her body. Then, almost silently, she began to cry.

"Hey, now," he soothed, wanting to comfort her but glad she was finally releasing all that pent-up emotion. He settled for snuggling closer, rocking her gently.

"D-don't tell me not to cry." Her voice was high-pitched, squeaky from the tears. "I'm not a weak, helpless female, but m-my son is h-hurt. My life is a horrible m-mess and I ruined m-my dress. Don't you dare t-tell me."

One corner of his mouth lifted with acute tenderness. She sounded ready to punch him out if he tried to shush her. "You go on and cry, P. Nothing weak about that. Let it out." He smoothed her curls slowly back from her temple and watched them spring back into place beneath his palm. A shot of 100-proof unadulterated love burned his throat. "I'll hold you. Okay?"

She nodded, her chest hiking with quick little intakes of breath. He held her as the tears seeped from the corners of her eyes and watched her press her lips together in a valiant effort to control them. Her tummy contracted and trembled beneath his palm. Every few moments, she blew out air and hiccuped more in.

"God, I h-hate crying."

He chuckled softly. The dim room smelled like her perfume and lemony tea, like green apple shampoo and woman. All the details he'd grown so accustomed to in the past fourteen years stood out in brash focus. Pilar—his wife, his *life*—had never felt more right in his arms.

She reached up and brushed tear trails from her ears, then whipped him a staccato glance before settling her head back into the crook of his shoulder and releasing a morose sigh. Taking a little gulp of air, she whispered, "Danny . . . I'm sorry."

Nervous hope jolted inside him. He worked hard to tamp down his thundering emotion before speaking. Swallowing once, he planted a kiss on her bare shoulder. "For what?"

"For not telling you. Not . . . t-talking to you. I don't know." She shifted in his arms until she could look up into his face, and he read contrition and vulnerability in her expression. "For letting things get worse and worse until there was just no turning back."

He smiled, loving her so much he shook with it. "There's always a place to turn back, and you don't have to apologize. I'm sorry I didn't ask you what was wrong. It's not my way, but I want to change. I will change. I'll . . ." his words caught on thick emotion. He clenched his jaw, fighting for control. "I'll do whatever it takes to be the man you want, if you'll just let me."

Her wet eyes searched his face for a long time, and then she sighed. "You've always been the man I want, Danny. Don't change too much." The words were a husky warble, an admission that had been difficult for her to make, he was sure.

He didn't know what to say.

In slow increments, she stilled, except for her chest above the plunging neckline of her nightgown. It rose and fell, rapidly at first, then gradually shallowing until he could detect small tremors of anticipation on her dusky rose flesh. The diamond pendant he'd given her when Pep made his squalling entrance into the world lay nestled in her shadowy cleavage. It rolled slightly with each hitched inhale and exhale. The room hummed with the pent-up desire between them, with the need, the sorrow, the desperation, the fear.

"Whatever you want, baby girl. Whatever it takes." His body responded to their fiery connection, and he wondered if she felt him hard against her. Wondered if it excited her, made her want him as much as he wanted her. "It can be okay if we want it to be."

He waited, but she didn't offer up any denials. Blood pounded in his neck as he marveled at the sheer, promising stillness of the moment. He dipped his head closer, testing, knowing if she pulled back, he'd die inside. He closed the distance with achingly slow movements. She didn't pull back.

Her gaze fluttered from his eyes to his mouth just as she raked that plump bottom lip between her teeth. A simple gesture, yet powerful and telling. It completely undid him.

With a groan from some sheltered masculine place deep inside, he leaned forward and captured her lips. Her lemon-scented breath rushed gently forth, and he drank it in, wanting to consume her, to meld with her. He kissed, nipped, loved her mouth and felt a hot stinging at the back of his eyes when she returned the attention with fervor. Her small capable hands found their way under the T-shirt he'd worn only out of respect for her, and his muscles contracted at her cool, feminine touch against his overheated skin. Her thumbs brushed his nipples, prompting a sharp hiss of an inhale from him. Desire swelled and burst inside his heart.

She explored his chest with tentative fingertips, caressing and pressing, grazing his flesh with her short nails. Her palms smoothed around to his back, and the embrace pillowed her breasts against him. As his tongue explored her mouth, he reveled in the feeling of silk over tightened nipples, her curves molding against his muscles. Hard and pulsing, he surrendered to his primal urge to thrust, pressing against the swell of her hip. She rewarded him with a moan, a suggestive turn toward him.

An agreement. Could it be?

His palm smoothed a route from shoulder to hip as he lifted his mouth from hers. "Pilar . . ."

"No, please." Her eyelids fluttered shut and she licked her lips. "Don't talk. Not now."

Warning nagged, but he cupped one side of her face and delved into her hot, inviting mouth once again, his thumb tracing the curve of her cheekbone. Could she only bear to make love to him if she didn't think about it? He couldn't take that. He had to know she loved and wanted him as much as he wanted her, and not just physically.

Maneuvering himself over her small body, he slipped one leg between hers, higher until his thigh met silk over moist heat. He pressed, and she writhed, pushing closer to the taunting pressure he knew she loved. He pulled his head back and watched her, his heart thudding in his chest. *Let me please you,* he thought as his thigh muscle flexed with the rhythm against her body. He needed to know he still could.

Eyes closed, she arched her head back and released a small moan, and the wellspring of raw need gushed inside him. He propped himself on one elbow and hooked his other hand under the hem of his T-shirt, yanking it over his head. His eyes devoured her as he tossed the shirt across the room, then shed his sleep boxers just as unceremoniously. Before he could settle back against her, her hand closed around his solid, pulsing erection with an unmistakable proprietary interest. Her warm palm caressed down, up, and down again, and a ragged moan broke loose from his chest. Up over the moist tip her hand slipped, and down the other side. He thought he might die from the acute pleasure.

When he couldn't bear another silky stroke, he fumbled around her intoxicating caresses and pushed the crumpled silk of her nightgown up her body until she was forced to release him so he could rid her of the intolerable barrier. It wasn't humanly possible to get as close to her as he wanted, but he'd damn well give it his best shot.

Hooking her thumbs in the sides of her bikinis, she raised her hips then pushed the underwear partway down, kicking them the rest. She reached for him with an urgency he hadn't seen in a long time. God, it felt incredible.

Covering her small body with his, he rained kisses on her collarbone and chest, tugging her nipples into his mouth with his lips and tongue as he cupped her breasts, lifting them to his mouth like a starving man. She groaned and twisted, the musky scent of her body wafting up to tease and entice him. He kissed the salty perspiration from between her breasts as his thumbs brushed her pearled nipples, scarcely able to think for the throbbing urgency to be inside her. It was a pure, singular need that eclipsed the rest of the world.

Smoothing his way up the insides of her arms, he guided her hands to the bars of the brass headboard and curved them around the posts, covering them with his own. He gazed down at her, then forced himself to stop touching, kissing, moving, going completely still until her eyes opened. She blinked up at him with a sweet combination of trepidation, vulnerability, and drugging desire.

"I'm going to make love to you," he half whispered, half growled. "Tell me now if that isn't what you want, P, and I'll stop."

She didn't answer, but he saw her shudder and felt the goose bumps on her skin. He slid his hands from her shoulders, over her breasts, down her stomach, and around to the soft, round flesh of her behind. Her eyes drifted closed again as he raised to his haunches between her legs and cupped her buttocks, lifting her body to him. His hard length rested flush against her wetness, but he held back. Soft thighs circled his hips, and he allowed a moment to feast his eyes on her achingly beautiful body. She was ready for him; he could see it, feel it. But he wanted her mind and heart ready as well as her body.

He repositioned himself until the tip of his erection probed her slick folds gently. She whimpered and bucked forward, but he held back, unwilling to enter her until he could read the expression in her eyes.

"Pilar. Baby girl, look at me."

Her eyelids raised to half mast, and she leaned her cheek shyly against her up-stretched arm.

He smiled gently, moving just barely in, then out of her body, slow and rhythmic. "Look at me when I make love to you, *querida*. I need you to see the love in my eyes. I have to know you want it, too."

Her chest rose and fell, her mouth slightly parted. After a moment, she moistened her lips with a flick of her tongue, and her eyelids drooped with provocative shyness. "I'm watching, D."

A tangled blast of pain and desire and connection and loss ripped through his chest, blurring the moment. She hadn't called him that in forever. With one solid thrust of possession, he pushed into her until her thighs strained against him. She cried out, and he leaned forward to cover her body, bracing his forearms next to her shoulders on the mattress. Breaths heaving, throbbing and rock-hard inside her, he kissed her mouth. "Did I hurt you, babe?" he asked, with considerable effort.

"No." She gave a demanding buck of her hips, forcing a grunt of raw pleasure from him. "You want me to watch you? Well, I don't want you to hold back. Please, not this time."

She didn't have to tell him twice. He withdrew and drove into her again. Again and again. She met him stroke for stroke, urging him on, harder and faster, with smoldering passion in her eyes and gasping sex-siren words rolling off her tongue. When he couldn't bear to hear one more hot suggestion without exploding, he stifled her words with his lips, sucking her tongue into his mouth as he plunged hard into her intoxicating wet silk. Her thighs tightened around his waist and her heels ground against his buttocks as they flexed. Sleek muscles in her arms tensed into relief as she braced herself with the headboard bars to meet his thrusts with answering power.

She teetered on the edge. He could feel it.

Breaking the kiss, he drank in the sight of her chest flushing almost purple with tension, her nipples puckering pebble-hard as goose bumps washed down her body. So hot. So tight. She began to clench and spasm around him, and his breath caught. Her eyes were closed. *No. Not yet.* "Look at me," he rasped through labored breaths. "Open your eyes." She did.

Locking with her gaze, he braced his hands above hers on the brass bars and leveraged himself into her body, hard, harder, faster. Through passion-clenched teeth, he grunted, "I won't let you go, Pilar. I can't. No one else will ever make love to you like this. . . ." Hot tears blurred his eyes as her body gripped fiercely. The power of her release nearly blinded him.

She cried out his name, shuddering against him again and again. His tears fell in glistening splatters on her face and neck. When her peak began to subside, he gave one final thrust, one hoarse groan, feeling as if his heart had disintegrated into a trillion glittering pieces and poured into her body in long, pulsating blasts. An illusion, he knew. She already had his heart and always would.

He lay panting and sweat-sheened above her, hands frozen around the bars above their heads, shaken as he was by the sheer emotional force of their joining. The bedclothes lay rumpled and twined around their ankles, but neither seemed inclined to move. He rested his forehead against hers, unmindful of his tears coursing down her temples.

They stayed in that position until their chests stopped heaving, until she stirred beneath his weight. His grip on the bars relaxed and he let his hands slide down and cover hers. All at once he felt it, and his heart jolted. Her wedding ring was back on her finger, where it belonged forever. *There was hope.*

He raised his face from hers, kissing the moisture from her cheeks. She stared up at him, her smile tremulous. Like a flash, he saw them back in high school, steaming his car windows opaque, loving each other with the ferocity and eagerness of discovery. A sweet ache filled him, and he said the only words that came to mind, the only appropriate statement for this moment.

"I love you, Pilar Valenzuela," he whispered. "Forever and a day."

Seven

From Pilar Valenzuela's journal, Tuesday, September 25:

Holy crap. What was I thinking?

After the languorous, post-lovemaking warmth had cooled in the wee morning hours, reality slammed down on Pilar like a guillotine—*thwack!* Heck yeah, she'd lost her head. She didn't regret making love with Danny—far from it. It had been the hottest, most intense sensory and emotional smorgasbord she'd gorged upon in forever, and she'd needed it desperately, especially last night. Every time she flashed back to it, her tummy flopped like a hooked and landed trout. One would think she and Danny were brand-new lovers, not long-time married folks. But, she didn't regret the lovemaking. Not a chance. What she did regret were the complications and assumptions their lovemaking would undoubtedly hurl into the already jumbled mix.

Her stomach jolted. Oh, God. It would be *so* easy to just give in, to welcome him home and try to block out the unhappiness that had pushed her to ask for divorce in the first place. But ignoring the truth would be about as effective as a Band-Aid over a stab wound. Facts were facts. As powerful as the passion had been, one night of world-class, gold-medal-winning, come-to-papa sex still didn't have the strength to erasc eight years of growing disillusionment. When the blinding glow of passion had faded, their problems remained, like hulking sentinels in the darkness. She needed Danny to see that, to accept it, but she sincerely doubted he would, considering her wanton behavior. Heat rose to her cheeks.

Híjola. Talk about sending mixed messages.

She'd told him not to change too much, for cripe's sake! Was she high?

Pilar plucked at the front of her nightgown with nervous fingers, fanning it out to cool her skin. Her dilemma, then, was figuring out how to explain her needs logically. She still wanted Danny to stay and help with the tight surveillance on Teddy, but that was all. No more sex to confuse the issue—not that she was interested. She snatched a coffee mug from the cupboard, filling it. *Liar.*

Okay, if she wanted to be completely honest with herself, she *was* interested, despite her better judgment. And she had to admit, though she hadn't believed it to be true, Danny still seemed fairly attracted to her. Okay—a lot attracted. A shudder crackled over her flesh like St. Elmo's fire at the memory of *just how much.*

Don't think about it.

She'd even go so far as to say her mind was now

open to the possibility of working things out with Danny. But *working* them out, as in, they weren't worked out yet, despite what last night's passion might indicate. Damn. She desperately needed to force last night's passion from her brain, heart, nerve endings so she could think straight, but it was proving a futile pursuit. All the more reason why they couldn't afford to get distracted again by such fiery, all-consuming, mind/body/soul-blitzing *sex*.

Don't think about it.

She sighed. Why did men always seem to think a rowdy session of stack and wiggle could solve everything from menstrual cramps to estrangement? Although she heartily wished sex were a magical cure-all, it wasn't. Not this time. But how would she make *him* see that without seeming as wishy-washy as she felt?

The nagging worry over this impossible tangle of contradictions had kept her wide-eyed and stiff-spined throughout the night as she considered and reconsidered the repercussions. Near dawn, she'd slipped from the warmth of the unexpectedly shared bed, desperate to steal some private moments and order her thoughts, organize the facts, and prepare her closing argument. Clarity, distance—she needed them. Common sense, self-restraint—*good luck, Pilar.*

She shot a glance at the clock and winced. Man, time flew when it was laced with dread. She'd be facing him, the jury of one, any minute now, and she had yet to banish the sensual memory of their tender-fierce lovemaking from her mind. Images flashed in her mind's eye like a sultry movie, complete with technicolor and surround sound.

Don't think about it.

Annoyed, she snagged the dishcloth and scoured the already immaculate countertop, simultaneously dreading and listening for Danny's footsteps in the hall. Fickle, that's what she was. Girl Most Likely to Waver in her Decisions. Girl Least Likely to Stick to her Guns. Girl Most Likely to Cave in at the First Sight of Danny Valenzuela's Sexy Bedroom Eyes and Bare-Muscled Chest.

Don't think about it.

No. She clenched her teeth. If she wanted him to believe and respect that she'd had enough of being taken for granted, she had to forget last night's pleasurable relapse and let him know where she truly stood the moment he entered the room. Just lay it right out—bam!—the world according to Pilar, no questions, no arguments, no hesitation. No wavering. And no more sex!

No one else will ever make love to you like this.

She sucked in a breath, letting her eyes drift closed. The vigorous scrubbing stilled, her fist clutching the damp cloth as though it were her last tenuous hold on reality. Danny's whispered words played over and over in her mind. From another man they may have sounded ominous, but from Danny, *her* Danny, they just sounded . . . true. And good.

So damn good. God, she wanted him again.

No! Don't think about it.

Despite valiant efforts to dam it, hot desire poured into her limbs like lava. She abandoned the dishcloth, dried her hands, then wrapped her numb fingers around the coffee cup she'd filled. Lifting it until the steam rose to warm her face, she gave herself a mental pep talk.

Buck up, Pilar. You can do this. She took a sip. No matter how delectable he looked or how he looked *at her,* she had to somehow make him understand that nothing had been instantaneously solved. She simply must stay in control. More than anything, she absolutely positively *had* to avoid ending up in his arms, in their bed, beneath him again—or she'd be a goner with a capital G.

Don't. Think. About. It!

A toilet flushed and a door hinge squeaked in the distance. Her glance jerked toward the hallway, stars spinning into her vision. Clunking the coffee cup down on the water-streaked countertop, she gripped the edge of the sink, ears perked like a cornered animal. Time out! She wasn't ready for this. Okay, wait. She closed her eyes and ordered herself to take a couple deep breaths. In . . . out. In . . . she heard Danny's voice, then Pep's, and she exhaled in a whoosh.

Just swell. One would think Pep would be a welcome buffer for this, their first conversation since . . . that thing she wasn't thinking about . . . but Pep had his own agenda. She'd have to confront her husband and her little parent trap watchdog all at once, both of them firing their Valenzuela charm at her with double barrels. *Outnumbered and outgunned.*

Closing her eyes, Pilar crossed herself and pressed a tight kiss to the side of her fist. She'd need more than prayer to resist her boys, but at least it was a start.

* * *

Hot damn. Dan was a man with a plan. Finally. And it felt almost as good as making love to Pilar had last night. Almost. "Go on down to the kitchen, son." He squeezed Pep's small shoulder. "I'm going to check on your brother."

"'Kay!"

Dan paused with his hand on Teddy's doorknob and watched his son pummel down the hallway. Dan's spirits were unusually high this morning, and—call him cocky—he just had to congratulate himself one more time for his brilliant plan to win Pilar back. As he'd lain awake trying to figure out how to keep her next to him in that bed where she belonged, the mother of all brainstorms had struck.

It had required all his self-restraint to fake sleep instead of jumping into action in the middle of the night, but he'd sensed Pilar was awake, too. He couldn't afford to pique her curiosity by leaping from bed and scurrying off through the dark house.

He allowed a moment to picture Pilar lying next to him, stiff as a board, drawing silent, shallow breaths. He smirked. She'd never been good at faking sleep. Clearly, she'd been worrying that he'd try to steamroll his way back into the marriage after their unexpected lovemaking, which—she'd be glad to know—wasn't part of the plan. Picturing their mind-altering passion again, his body tightened.

Don't think about it.

With a grimace, he adjusted his sleep boxers as best he could. No doubt Pilar had rocked his world, and yes, the memories made him hot. But he had to keep his mind out of his shorts and on the matter at hand.

It was up to him to convince Pilar that he planned to let her take the lead, so it wouldn't do for him to saunter into the kitchen arousal first. He stood in the hallway until his body settled, then crept into Teddy's room to check him before facing his wife.

The curtains were drawn, cloaking the room in cool darkness. Teddy slept like a rock, breathing deeply and looking peaceful. Dan didn't have the heart to wake him, so he settled for tucking the quilt up higher around his little shoulders.

As he tiptoed toward the door, Dan caught sight of the journal he'd returned to the exact position he'd found it last night. A slow smile spread across his face. He hadn't read much of it, just the past few days' worth. Enough to plant the idea in his subconscious. Enough to know that Pilar wasn't as dead set on this divorce as she seemed, she just didn't know her way back to the place where they were partners and life was good. But as painful as it had been for him to read her anguished, conflicted words, they made him realize there was still room to change her mind, and doing so was his responsibility. His resolve strengthened.

At first he hadn't a clue as to how to do it. Lying there imprisoned in insomnia, he'd run through all the conversations he'd had about or with Pilar since the split. The nonsensical notions had swirled around in his mind like those refrigerator poetry magnets, offering no insight. But finally the words began to form logical thoughts, and the thoughts eventually led to Dan's Brilliant Plan.

You forgot me. That's what I can't live with . . .
Were you attentive?

What about cherish? Did you forget that?
You won her once, Dan. How did you do it?

Oh, yeah. This had to work. The key to winning Pilar back, he'd decided, was written inside her high school journal tucked away somewhere in this house. His glimpse inside her current diary taught him one important fact: his wife faithfully logged every minute life detail and her feelings about them. So if he could find the journals she'd kept during their courtship back in high school and discover what he'd done right the first time, all he had to do was repeat the steps. Right? If it ain't broke, don't fix it. God, it was inspired. Of course, he didn't know how Pilar would feel when she learned that he'd read her journals, but . . .

Definitely don't think about it.

Naturally, Teddy's recuperation was first priority. But while he was living in the house, Dan also intended to unearth that journal without Pilar suspecting. Before he could search, however, he had to ease her mind about last night. No pressure—that was his new motto. He was the rookie in this partnership, and the sooner she knew he felt that way, the sooner she'd drop her guard. He wasn't giving up; he was going with the force instead of resisting it, one of the basic principles of combat. Not that this was war. It was love.

But the sooner he could find that journal and plan his action, the sooner Pilar would be his again. Just like last night—only this time it would be forever. His breath caught.

Don't think about it.

* * *

Pilar's heartbeat pounded like a reggae drum solo by the time a sleep-tousled Pep rounded the corner and sought her out. She expected Danny to appear at his heels, but he didn't. She didn't know whether to be relieved or worried.

"Good morning, *hijito.*" She opened her arms, and Pep ran across the tile floor and folded himself against her.

"Hi, Mama."

Her tension eased a notch from the hug. She bent and planted a kiss on top of his head. "Where's Daddy?"

"Checkin' on Teddy Bed-wetty." His eyes raised imploringly. "Do I gotta go to school today?"

"Hmmm. We had a pretty scary night." She narrowed her gaze and twisted her mouth to the side as though contemplating it. "I think you can take a mental health day."

"Yes!" He extracted himself from her embrace and pumped his arm, boinging around the kitchen like he'd just made the game-winning touchdown. "Can I have Twinkies for breakfast?"

She blurted a little laugh. "Quit while you're ahead, bug."

He giggled and dragged a kitchen chair to the cereal cupboard, climbing up on it. Before opening the door to peruse his choices, he turned toward her for one more negotiation attempt, wagging his finger. "Okay, cereal, but I get to eat it on the TV tray in the living room and watch cartoons, even though it's not Saturday. Pleeease?"

His teasing persuasion was hard to resist. Why not?

He deserved a little reward for his bravery. Besides, having him out of earshot would make it easier for her and Danny to get over the most awkward part of this unintended morning after. Ugh! "Okay, but you know the rules. If you spill, I'm gonna have Daddy hang you upside down and clean it with your hair."

Pep gaped, his eyes gleaming. Clearly the idea of becoming a human mop intrigued him. "Nuh-uh!?"

She tickled behind his knee, favoring him with her most playful threatening scowl. "Just don't spill."

"'Kay." He opened the cupboard and planted his fists on his hips, eyes searching the multicolored boxes while he made little clicking noises with his cheek. Finally he pulled out the Cheerios and hugged them to his chest. "What's Teddy gonna eat now that he has jack-o'-lantern teeth?"

"Pep, I don't want you teasing your brother, okay? His jaw will be sore and he's probably self-conscious about his missing teeth. Promise me you won't tease. I'm not kidding."

"O-ookay, man!" Pep rolled his eyes.

She picked up her coffee mug and sipped, considering Pep's question. "I think I'll make him a fruit smoothie. That should go down pretty easily. Would you like one, too?"

Pep retrieved a bowl, then jumped from the chair and fished a spoon out of the drawer. As he headed toward the living room with his spoils, he answered over his shoulder. "Yep, with a strawberry on top. Pretty please, thank you." He shot her a charming grin. "I'll yell when I'm ready."

With permission, the boys could occasionally eat

breakfast in front of the television: it was a house rule. But either she or Danny would come pour the milk, and it had to be all gone before the boys could carry their dishes back into the kitchen. Strict, perhaps, but it got them to finish all their milk, and it also saved her carpeting from ruin.

"Not too loud. Teddy's sleeping." She watched him go with a smile on her face, her earlier panic almost completely gone. Pep seemed so carefree this morning, more so than he'd been since . . . she sighed. Since Danny had left.

Her anxiety resumed. She still had to face her husband. Setting her coffee aside, she pulled open the refrigerator and bent to ferret through their fruit and yogurt selections. Teddy wasn't as picky as he'd been a few years earlier, thank goodness. Green leafy vegetables were still the enemy, but he'd made peace with most fruits.

She had some strawberries and raspberries, a few clementines, an apple, an Asian pear, and two bananas. She'd have to go to the store later and restock, and made a mental note to pick up pudding and Jell-O and some other soft foods. Gathering the fruit and a tub of vanilla yogurt against the front of her nightgown, she straightened carefully and shut the door.

And there stood Danny.

"Oh!" The fruit tumbled and bounced, rolling in a million different directions across the floor. Pilar managed to keep her grip on the yogurt.

Danny's eyebrow raised as his eyes tracked the pandemonium. He winked at her playfully. "Good morning, Carmen Miranda. I believe you dropped your hat."

Her throat tightened at the feel of his voice against her skin, like a rough, promising caress. "Very funny."

He bent to retrieve the spilled goods while she just stood there clutching the front of her gown like a twit, staring down at him. What ever happened to staying in control? To keeping the upper hand? Heat swirled over her skin as she watched him. The muscles in his shoulders bunched and stretched through his T-shirt. Dark hair swirled over his bare, muscular, brown legs, the very same legs that had— ugh! She couldn't do this to herself. "I-I'm making a fruit smoothie for Teddy," she blurted.

"Good idea, but it's easiest if you put the fruit in the blender instead of squishing it all over the floor." He stood and loaded everything onto the counter, a smirk on his face.

"Well"—she sniffed haughtily—"you scared me, is all." She turned to the sink and began to rinse the fruit under the faucet with jerky, nerve-shot movements. In her peripheral vision, she watched Danny pull a coffee mug from the cupboard and fill it. He leaned one hip against the counter next to her, and she ceased breathing. Good thing, because he was too close, and she could smell his masculine, sleep-musked skin, which was more than her willpower could handle.

"I never meant to scare you, P." The words were a low, throaty purr. "Not this morning, and not last night. And on that note, I think we should talk."

Whoa! An involuntary squeeze shot the small

green apple she'd been washing straight up into the air. Danny reached out easily and palmed it, handing it back without a single smart alec comment. Thank God for small favors. She took it with a shaky hand, barely able to meet his inquisitive eyes. "Yes. We do need to talk, because—"

"Me first," Danny interjected. "Please."

A sigh breezed from her lips. What the hell? If the erupting fruit was any indication, she didn't really have her wits about her at the moment anyway. So much for her big assertiveness plans. "Okay. Go ahead."

"Let me get it all out before you say anything." He sipped his coffee, then set the cup aside, pinning her with an earnest gaze. "I'm gonna jump right in. I don't want us to read too much into what happened, P. That would make things awkward, considering we still have so many issues to deal with. You know?"

Holy—Stunned. She was stunned. She hadn't expected *that* at all, and now she couldn't even blink, much less process his words through her slow-motion brain. Make things awkward? Too many issues?

"Pilar?"

She started. *Answer him!* "Uh, y-yes. I agree."

He nodded. "Good." His voice lowered to a sultry growl. "We needed each other last night, and nothing's wrong with that. We're husband and wife. We shouldn't feel guilty for, well"—he cleared his throat and smiled almost bashfully—"for, ah . . . you get my drift, right?"

Forget blinking; she couldn't breathe. Had she

heard him right? He didn't want them to feel guilty for making love? He wasn't going to push the issue? *Who are you, and what have you done with my husband?*

"Pilar?" he prompted.

"Huh? Oh. Yes. I-I, um, drift. Got it." God, did she ever. Her gaze dropped to his lips of their own volition, and desire swirled in her stomach.

"Anyway, my point." He swiped his palms together. "While Teddy recuperates, I think it'd be best if I slept in the guest room. That way there will be no confusion, no added tension. Okay?"

The . . . guest room? "W-what did you say?"

Looking cool and calm in direct contrast to her blathering astonishment, he retrieved and sipped his coffee. After swallowing and brushing the back of his hand over his lips, he added, "I said, I think it would be best if we stuck to our original agreement. Me in the guest room until Teddy is better. You in our bed."

Was it her imagination, or had his voice sounded like stonewashed velvet when he added the "you in our bed" part? But wait a minute—he was telling her exactly what she'd planned to tell him. No way! Esme claimed men weren't mind readers, but maybe some of them were. Still, Danny Valenzuela? Preposterous. Her hand fluttered up to twist her pendant in her fist, a bad nervous habit she needed to break before she broke the chain instead. "But, I . . . thought . . ."

"You disagree?" He cocked an eyebrow. "That's a surprise. But if you think we should share a bed, I guess—"

"No! No. I just . . ." She clamped off her words and studied his face for signs of an ulterior motive, but found nothing but sincerity in his expression. This was too good to be true. Maybe there was hope. She released a sigh of tension. "Thank you, Danny. I worried you'd think . . ."

"Ah!" He held up his palm and turned his face as if to halt her words. When he looked back at her, a slow, sexy smile cut into his whisker-darkened cheeks. "No assumptions, from here on out." He paused, then headed for the fridge. "Deal?"

She laughed softly and shook her head. "Deal."

This was gonna be great, Danny thought, closing the fridge without removing anything from it. He'd needed the full-frontal cold blast before he did something stupid with his sexily touseled but strictly off-limits wife. With cartoon sounds carrying in from the living room, he settled against the refrigerator door and watched her wash the fruit. He had seen the tension drain from her once she realized he didn't intend to chain her up as his unwilling—or willing—sexual captive.

A carefree smile lifted Dan's lips, but then she reached for a chopping knife, and the movement drew his gaze to the smooth skin above the vee-back of her nightgown. A feeling of hungry male appreciation replaced his smile, and his willful mind cast Pilar in the role of his willing sexual captive.

Just like that, he was propelled back to last night. Desire ripped through him, and the floor beneath him bucked and undulated. She was so beautiful. He wanted her. Wanted to squeeze that orange she was peeling over her chest and lick the tangy juice off her nipples. He may have committed himself to the plan, but he couldn't resist moving up behind and caging her between his arms and the counter.

Her motions stilled, and for a moment he just watched her breath hitch and her hands quiver. Unwilling to push his luck too far, he nuzzled through her hair until his lips grazed her ear. Her sharp intake of breath seemed to move through her into him, settling low and heavy and hot. "Just so there's no doubt in your mind, I meant every word I said last night. All in due time, baby girl."

Her lips parted as though she planned to speak, but before she had mustered a response—

"Got milk?" Pep cried out, apparently ready for someone to fix his cereal. Dan laughed, but Pilar whirled in his arms, eyes searching for escape.

"Let me . . . I need to . . ." The telltale hot flush rose on her chest. "I-I should—"

"I'll get him." Dan sauntered lazily away from Pilar and her kissable lips and retrieved the milk. Thank God Pep had intervened, Dan thought, with the precious few blood cells that hadn't left his brain for the quick vacation south. His actions had been just about ready to contradict his promises, which wouldn't do much for his plan. He swaggered out of the kitchen, but couldn't resist tossing an innuendo-laden parting shot over his shoulder from the archway. "Hey, I'm glad we talked, Punkybean."

Eight

From Pilar Valenzuela's journal, Monday, October 1:

I can't believe it's October already, or that a week has passed since Teddy's accident. Thank God he's a resilient little bugger. He's doing great. It's getting harder keeping him still, though, and he can't roughhouse for at least another week. I never thought that boy would grow tired of TV and computer games, but miracles do exist, I've learned.

Speaking of miracles . . . Danny, a.k.a. the Merry Maid, formerly known as my absentee husband. What is up with him? In addition to taking his share of turns watchdogging Teddy every day, he has mysteriously morphed into Mr. Clean. No exaggeration. He's been going like the Energizer Bunny since last Tuesday, and I just can't figure it out. I'm not referring to the regular stuff, like caulking the bathtub or replacing lightbulbs. Danny has been doing some major cleaning. He not only organized all the closets, scoured the garage, and rearranged the basement, but right now he's up cleaning out the attic, of all things. The attic! It's like the more he digs around, the more he wants to. Freaky. At first I thought he was looking for something, but he said he's just straightening up. Weird. Not that I'm complaining.

It's been so nice having him home. Really *home, not like before. I only wish it could be like this all the time, but I know that's a pipe dream. This week's been a false honeymoon.*

Blech. Bad choice of words.

Me<---skeptic.

I want to believe. But if history is any indication, sooner or later reality's gonna send me that check.

Standing next to the hanging ladder, Pilar peered up into the sharply angled wood-beamed attic. Dust motes floated in the wan glow from the portable work light Danny had carried up, its thick orange cord dangling through the hole like a long lizard's tail. Muffled scratches wafting down from some back corner she couldn't see told her she either had big rats or her husband was hard at work. "Danny?"

She winced at the ensuing sounds of items being dropped and Danny's muffled swear words. Oops. Gray dust rained down on her when Danny's jeans-clad legs moved into her line of sight through the square opening. She backed up and waved her hand in front of her, coughing, then glanced up again, shading her eyes. The closet light succeeded in illuminating the bottom half of him, but his face remained in the shadows. She craned her neck. "I can't see you."

He squatted at the opening, worry lining his dirt-smeared face. "Sorry." He grimaced as more debris tumbled down. "What's up? Teddy okay?"

"He's fine. Restless, though." She brushed a cob-web from her arm, then propped her foot on the bottom rung. "You've been up there forever. How much longer, do you think?" Man, did her words have to come out sounding so codependent?

"Oh, uh . . ."

He shot a glance over his shoulder, at what, Pilar couldn't guess. It had been years since she'd ventured into the attic.

"Let me straighten up. Half an hour or so. You going somewhere?"

"No, but your mom's stopping by, and . . ." She shrugged, not wanting to admit she felt uncomfortable being alone with Rosario. She dreaded thinking of her mother-in-law's probable opinion of their situation. They'd missed the annual Broncos-Raiders family football party, and though Teddy's accident had served as the perfect excuse, Pilar was sure the whole family knew by now. She could just imagine the smoking phone lines between her curious sisters-in-law. The thought of being grist for the gossip mill turned her stomach.

The familiar war of mixed feelings waged within her heart. Things were so off-kilter. Since they'd made love, she and Danny had slipped into a warily comfortable routine of living like polite strangers. It wasn't a marriage, but it was better than it had been just before she'd asked him to leave. Having him here was comforting, though, and every so often she had an urge to tell him to stay. She didn't know if she had the strength to disrupt the family again.

But that would be settling, wouldn't it? Could she live with herself if she settled? Then again, could she live with the guilt if she didn't?

". . . down in a sec," she heard Danny say. Her eyelids fluttered as she redirected her attention. "I'm sorry, what?"

"I said, I'll be down in a sec." He cocked his head and frowned with concern. "You OK?"

"Yeah, I'm just . . . I don't know." Her eyes drifted to the semidarkness behind him. Though wary of the future, the truth was she'd been missing him all morning. And ever since she'd taken a certain phone message earlier, the deceptively safe cocoon they'd spun seemed on the brink of collapse. She wanted to hang on.

Unable to think of anything meatier, Pilar cleared her throat and nodded toward the dusty abyss. "Making progress?"

"Well, uh . . . not as much as I'd hoped. It's a mess up here." Unexplained wry humor danced in his eyes.

"So I see. Find any treasures amongst the cobwebs?"

A rather sick little smile curved his lips. "Not yet, but I haven't given up hope." He clapped his palms together, sending another warren of dust bunnies hopping. "Well, the sooner I can get through this, the sooner I'll be down."

"Okay. Um . . ." She ran her fingers through her hair and stared at the wall, thinking of the phone call. Now or never. It wasn't fair or reasonable to hide it from him. She couldn't keep reality at bay forever.

Tilting her head back, she met his gaze directly. "Nora Obermeyer called. She said she was returning your call."

Realization flickered, then faded, in his eyes. "Oh,

good." She waited for him to elaborate. Naturally, he didn't. Instead he averted his gaze. "I'll call her when I'm done. Thanks."

Bitterness surged. So he wasn't gonna tell her squat, was that it? She should've known. *Let it drop, Pilar.* She really should. The man had responsibilities, after all. But why the furtiveness? Why couldn't they discuss things like a couple? She huffed. Just another barb-edged reminder that they still *weren't* a couple in some ways that really counted.

That all-too-familiar pain of abandonment clouded her common sense. She didn't even try to keep the wounded tone from her cutting words. "Itching to get back to work, now that you're stuck here with me and the boys?"

"It's not that, P." He sounded defeated, like he'd expected—and dreaded—this very reaction from her.

The fact that she was so predictable bothered her. "What then?" she snapped.

He studied her, lines of worry bracketing his mouth. "Listen to yourself. It's all there."

She frowned, confused. "What is?"

"Doubt. Resentment. Anger. Things will never heal between us until you trust that I can be less of a . . . a workaholic. My word means nothing to you"—he held up a hand when she opened her mouth to protest—"and I understand that. But I can't regain your trust until I go back to work and prove myself, P, so why prolong the agony, to use your words."

She set her jaw. Jerk. He had a point. She didn't want him to have one, because it made her look like a shrew. She really wanted to be the reasonable adult in all this, not the snippy, bitter wife. And she was doing so well . . . not.

"We've made some progress, Pilar, but nothing's settled. We both need to know where we're headed." He paused, the silence yawning between them. His earnest look dared her to deny it. "Am I right?"

Pilar wrapped her arm through the rungs and leaned her face against the ladder. At least he admitted his workaholism. That was something. "I guess." She couldn't help but fear that their tentative connection would unravel the minute he donned that uniform and returned to his first love—the job. The thought of being hurt again terrified her. She wanted to lash out now just to protect her heart from the inevitable pain.

"I have to work, P." His voice was a patient purr. "We need money to live."

"I know," she bit out, prompting a wave of guilt. Damn. If she wanted him to communicate with her, she should extend him the same courtesy. Checking the attitude in her voice, she sighed. "I'm sorry. It's just . . . things are improving, like you said. I worry you'll revert—"

"Pilar," he interrupted, his tone laced with gentle skepticism. "This week's been nice, yes. But you have to admit, it hasn't been a marriage." He spread his arms. "We're not even sleeping together. Is that how you want forever to look?"

Her stomach clenched. "I . . . want to work things out. I'm just scared."

"I know you are. Still, I can't just be your roommate. I want to be your husband and lover, but not until you accept me completely." A pause. "That won't happen until you're no longer scared. Until you trust me. You've gotta give me a fighting chance."

She chewed the inside of her cheek, grudgingly admiring his effort. Offering him an olive branch of sorts, she muttered, "You sound pretty convinced that you can."

"I am." His expression segued from frustration to guarded playfulness with a single wink. "Now I just have to convince you."

Hope floated inside her, but disappeared just as quickly. The path of least resistance would be sucking it up and letting him stay. The easiest path often led to most dissatisfaction, unfortunately, and she could not bear to settle for less than she deserved any longer. He was trying, she'd give him that. But did he have it in him to change for the long haul? She supposed he was right—she would never know unless she let go. So, fine. She would. But fear made her lift her chin and drill him with a stare. "Whether you go back right away or not, I can't make you any promises."

"I'm not asking for promises. All I want's a chance." He stilled then, waiting for her acquiescence. When she remained silent, he added, "You and the boys are the most important part of my life, but work is a part of it, too. I won't let it get in the way again." He sat on the edge of the attic entryway and reached his hand down.

After a moment of staring at it, remembering it touching her body, admiring the subtle shine of his worn wedding band against the brown skin, Pilar stepped up a rung and slid her palm into his. He rubbed her knuckles with his thumb and smiled. Her heart beat so hard, she couldn't do more than stare back.

"I love you so much, P, and I don't want to settle any more than you do. If you find you can't trust me one hundred percent, can't believe in me . . ." He pressed his lips together for a moment, unable or unwilling to complete the thought. "Please try, baby girl."

"I-I am trying. It's not that easy."

He squeezed her fingers gently. "I'm not asking for favors. I need you to trust me because you *do*, not just because I want it."

Shoot. Did she dare believe? She wanted to, with every fiber of her soul. In a moment of weakness, she blurted, "You know, you don't have to leave again." She cleared her throat, feeling faint. "We can . . . figure something out."

"No, babe," he whispered. "Not until you can welcome me back as your husband. You ready for that?" Her silence was a clear answer. The corner of his lip twitched. "When you're ready, not before. Ruben doesn't mind me staying there."

She swallowed thickly. "But the boys need you here."

Pain pulsed like lightning over his expression. "The boys." After a long pause, he blew out a controlled breath. "Fine. I'll stay for the boys. In the guest room. But things have to change between me and you if I'm going to stay for the long run. I can't bear to see resignation in your eyes every time I look at you."

"I-I know."

"Which is why I have to go back to work."

She sagged, accepting it. "Okay."

One eyebrow quirked. "Okay?"

Damn. One little brow waggle and she wanted to make love to him—right here, right now. Dust bunnies and dirt be damned, she yearned for him to convince her he really, truly meant what he said. He was warm and masculine and . . . Danny. So beautiful. She tried for a haughty tone. "What part of *okay* don't you understand?"

He laughed softly, gazing at her with so much love it stole her breath. Soon his expression darkened into something earthier, full of promise. She thought he might pull her up and kiss her, but the peal of the doorbell tore through the tenuous electricity crackling between them.

Pilar snatched her hand away, anxiety flooding her. "Oh no, that's your mother."

He shook his head like she'd gone crazy. "It's my *mom*, not the grim reaper. She loves you, remember?"

"Maybe she did—but now?" *Ding-dong.* Pilar looked at the doorway, feeling sick. "You did tell her, right?"

"Yes. Stop worrying."

"But, what exactly did she say when—?"

"Pilar, I told you. She—"

"Mama!" hollered Teddy from the living room.

"Shoot. I don't want Teddy riled up. Just hurry, please?"

"Hey. It'll be fine. We're family. We've been family for a long time, and that hasn't changed."

She didn't respond. Couldn't. But God, how she yearned for his words to be true.

Pilar had managed small talk, coffee, and more than her fair share of nervous gestures since greeting her mother-in-law in the foyer. Now if she could just shake this complete intimidation . . .

She glared daggers at the ceiling. Where the hell was Danny?

She'd left Rosario in the living room to baby Teddy like only an *abuelita* could, grateful for the space and time to catch her breath, but it passed all too quickly. She peered up as Rosario bustled through the archway and smiled across the cutaway kitchen counter. The thermal coffee carafe and thick mugs were on the table, and Pilar was almost done slicing the banana bread Esme'd brought over the day before. She managed an overbright excuse for a smile.

"Have a seat. The coffee's fresh." God. She felt so falsely cheery, like some pinafore-wearing superwife wannabe from a blighted episode of *Leave it to Beaver.* Her inane words came in a rapid-fire tumble she didn't seem able to control. "Danny will be down in a sec. He's been cleaning, well, everything. The basement, the closets, now the, uh, the attic. I can't figure it out." She blurted a dumb little laugh, her movements flighty as a hummingbird. Desperation treated her to a virtual lobotomy.

Help, I'm talking and I can't shut up!

"Anyway, Esme brought this bread, which goes really well with the coconut coffee. She makes great banana bread. I need to get the recipe, I keep telling myself. Give me a minute, I'll—oh, I have butter. Do you want jam, too?"

"Ah, *mi hija.*" The other woman's lined, bronze face warmed with compassion and . . . regret? She turned a chair from the table to face the kitchen and sank into it, smoothing the skirt of her plaid cotton shirtwaist. "Don't be so nervous around me, honey. I've known you since you were a girl. Marriages have problems." She pursed her lips. "I know my boys aren't the easiest men to live with."

Yikes, straight to the bone. Pilar sighed. What could she say? You're right? Your son's a pain in my butt, but I love him anyway? "I'm sorry. I don't mean to . . ."

"They had a hard time with their father being gone." Rosario's attention was focused on some distant memory that faded the normally bright light in her eyes like a day-old corsage. "I tried my best, but . . ." She shrugged, letting the half-statement stand.

Pilar felt a kick in the chest. Rosario shouldn't shoulder any blame. "You did a wonderful job raising them. None of this is your fault."

"Nonsense. I'm his mother." One black eyebrow arched. "You're saying he got all his traits from Victor's side? You wanna put me in an early grave?"

"Of course not, but Danny's a grown man." Pilar stacked the banana bread on a plate and pulled two butter knives from the drawer. "He makes his own decisions."

"That doesn't keep me from feeling bad that there are problems, or from praying that you and

Danielito work through them and stay together, *amada*. He needs you."

Ugh. Guilt trip, boarding here. Watch your step and carry your own baggage. "Well, we need him, too. But—"

"You need all of him, no?"

"Y-yes. I haven't had all of Danny since—"

"The boys were born," Rosario finished.

Surprise zinged through Pilar. "How did you—?"

"I understand more than you think." Rosario winked. "I'm his mother, but I'm also a woman."

Pilar's heart swelled with humble gratitude. She should've known Danny's mother would be reasonable. Rosario knew Danny better than anyone save Pilar herself. "I don't want to speak badly about your son, though. I respect you too much for that."

"Talking it out isn't the same as talking badly." Rosario sighed. "I make no claims that my boys are perfect."

Pilar chewed her lip. "Well, one problem, the man's got a one-track mind: work. It doesn't leave a whole lot of room for me and my needs."

The older woman clucked her tongue. "Ay, that boy. He wants to give of himself, Pilar. He just tries too hard sometimes and doesn't stop to figure out what other people need instead of what he *thinks* they need. He's always been that way. And, now, with the boys. I'm sure he's trying to be a better father than his was."

Pilar frowned. "Of course he's a better father than Victor. How could he even think otherwise?"

Rosario gave an enigmatic shrug. "Who knows what goes on in someone's head?"

Pilar carried the bread to Rosario, then plunked her elbows on the table and supported her chin with her palms. "Men are so annoying. Especially Valenzuela men."

Her mother-in-law laughed and stirred some thick, white *crema* into her coffee. "I know that more than most, *hija*. I married and divorced one and raised five more. But, Danny—that one's got a good heart. He's terrified to lose you. That's why he spins his wheels so much."

Pilar chewed her bottom lip, fighting not to cave in under the weight of her respect for this woman. "But spinning his wheels is what's pushing me away. I want to work things out. I do. But I can't just forgive him his faults and endure anymore."

"*Claro*. I'm not suggesting you stay if you're unhappy." Rosario's clear, dark eyes danced away. She toyed with her napkin. "I just hoped to help you understand him better, so maybe you could find compassion."

"We all have issues from childhood, mine being the fact that I was raised to make my bed and lie in it. But I don't want a 1950s marriage, Rosi. No offense to your generation of women." She sighed. "We have to choose to change patterns from childhood if they aren't working anymore."

"Oy-yoy-yoy . . . I know, honey." Rosi sipped.

"Danny needs to compromise. That's all I'm saying." She twisted her mouth, pleading for understanding. "I need him completely or not at all."

"*Sí.*" Rosario leaned forward and covered Pilar's hand with her own. "Find a chance for him in your heart, *mi hija*. It's not fair of me to ask that, but I love you both, and the boys." She shrugged an apology. "Frankly, I'm getting too old to care about convention. I just want my children happy, and Danny"—she laughed dryly—"that one needs you to be happy, Pilar. A mother knows."

Pilar smiled, realizing finally that she had an ally in Rosario, not a foe. "I'm trying."

"Don't misunderstand me, little one. I'm not telling you to compromise your needs. I just pray you and Danny don't give up too soon. For the boys as much as for yourselves."

Pilar's throat ached, and she looked away, picking at the crust of the banana bread for which she had no appetite. "I'm . . . not giving up. I still love him, Rosi—"

"*Bueno!* That's all I need to know," Rosario cut in, spreading her palms out flat to signal the end of the explanations. She wore a smug cat-who-ate-the-canary look. "The rest is God's will and your business." She nodded with finality. "How about some of that bread, hmm?"

Jackpot.

Given his limited time, Dan had launched into the final few minutes of journal hunting with the fervor of a gambling addict on his last roll of quarters. Luckily, it had paid off. *Ka-ching!* He stared down at the box marked "journals" with excitement building in his chest. He no longer cared about the cobwebs clinging to his skin, his sore muscles, or the dust coating his lungs. He'd found them at last.

Naturally he'd find them in the very last place he looked. Had he started this hunt in the attic, he wouldn't have had to suffer through cleaning all those closets. Or the garage. Not to mention the basement.

But it didn't matter, because here they were, and as a bonus, Pilar thought he was some kind of broom-toting knight in shining armor for dejunking the house. Teddy was on the mend, life was calming down, and soon he'd have the answers he needed to win his wife back.

He snapped open the blade of his folding Spyderco knife, kneeling carefully to slit the sealing tape. Setting the knife aside, he lifted the cover, which stirred up another dust devil. Turning his head, he sneezed twice, then his watering eyes sought the prize. The priceless book of answers. The jour—

Oh, no. His excitement fizzled like a birthday candle dropped in the bathtub. There had to be a hundred journals in this box. Why'd she have to be so damned prolific? Blowing out a frustrated sigh, Dan looked away, rubbing his knuckles across the edge of his jawline thoughtfully.

What now, Einstein? No way could he stay up here long enough to find the one he needed. Hell, he didn't even *know* which one he needed. His mother had been here more than half an hour, and Pilar was no doubt fuming because he hadn't shown his face. The last thing he wanted was to let her down *again*. Pissing her off probably wasn't the best way to

launch his grand plan, either. Not to mention that
he felt certain Pilar's curiosity—or annoyance—
would eventually send her up that drop ladder. The
thought of getting busted before he even began settled it.

Replacing the cover, Dan camouflaged the box
and started down the ladder toward the sounds of
Pilar's and his mother's voices in the kitchen. This
unexpected obstacle rankled, but he tried to stave
off the annoyance. Just a minor setback.

He'd have to resort to plan B . . . Esme and Lilly.

They were women, not to mention Pilar's best
friends. Surely they'd remember what journal Pilar
had used in high school. He hadn't wanted to in-
volve anyone else, but he needed a hand. The trick
would be convincing them to help . . . *and* to keep
the secret from Pilar. Could he do it?

Dan arrived at Common Grounds coffee shop
early, grateful he'd been able to get away from the
house. Relief had flowed through him when he'd
entered the kitchen to find Pilar and his mother
chatting away like always. He offered to grocery
shop while they visited, and—thank God—he'd
reached Esme and Lilly, who agreed to meet him
right away.

Lenny Kravitz crooned in the background of the
brick-walled coffee shop, and the smell of fresh-
ground Jamaican beans and pungent spices hung in
the air. Two dapper white-haired gentlemen played
checkers by the front window. A woman tapped away

on her laptop against the wall. A young couple sat losing themselves in each other's eyes at the round-top table nearest the bookshelves.

Dan ordered a house coffee—black—and waited by the counter until the server, a multipierced young man wearing a hemp shirt, baggy jeans, and seven woven wristbands, was done helping other customers.

One of his bejeweled eyebrows raised. "Did I forget something?" His hands worked with efficiency over the coffeemaker's many gleaming parts.

"No, just a request. I'm looking for two women. A petite pregnant lady and one who looks like a supermodel."

The man smirked, squinting as steam rose in his face. "I can respect your dream, dude, but this is a coffee shop, not Fantasy Island."

Dan barked a laugh. "No, these are actual women. I guess I should've said, I'm *expecting* them." He jerked his thumb over his shoulder. "Can you tell them I'm in the back?"

"Sure thing. A pregnant lady and a supermodel," he mumbled wryly, finishing off a *cappuccino* with a flourish of whipped cream. "That'll be hard to miss."

A few minutes later, Esme and Lilly entered the back room, each holding thick ceramic mugs.

"What's with that guy up front?" Lilly asked. "We walked in and I swear he laughed out loud at us."

"Probably caffeine overdose." Dan stood, taking their cups while they removed their jackets and settled in. "Thanks for meeting me. I'm sorry I called at the last minute."

"No problem." Esme smiled. "How's Teddy?"

"Bouncing back like a boomerang." They'd been lucky on that count.

"Kids are so hardy. *Pobrecito.*" Lilly tossed her hair and then rested her elbows on the table. "So, what's urgent, Danny V.?"

Lilly, he realized, would be the harder sell. "I need information." His heart pounded.

Lilly looked skeptical.

"Tell us." Esme interlaced her fingers over her belly.

He looked from one to the other. "Do you know when Pilar fell in love with me?"

A confusion-thick pause ensued.

"Um . . . Danny?" Lilly said, as though he were several colors short of a full crayon box. "We all went to school together, if you'll recall. Of course we know."

He shook his head. "I meant, exactly *when* did she fall in love with me? I need to know."

"Oh. Tenth grade," Lilly told him, just as Esme said, "Definitely our junior year."

Lilly peered quizzically at her. "You think it wasn't until junior year? They were together most of tenth."

Esme wagged her index finger. "Yeah, but then Pilar's dad made them break up for the summer before eleventh, remember?"

Dan groaned. "I sure as hell remember."

Esme smiled, then continued her explanation to Lilly as though he wasn't there. "That summer apart was what sealed it for Pea. They hadn't reached point of sale until after that, remember? Pea was still unsure. Junior year, he turned into Mister Charming—"

"Yes, then." Danny leaned forward, a spark of

hope inside him. Two pairs of eyes met his. "That's what I want. The year I was . . . uh . . ."

"Mister Charming? Eleventh grade." Esme nodded, certain.

"Now that I think about it, Es is right."

Dan cleared his throat. "You don't happen to remember what journal Pilar used then, do you?"

"Ugly neon swirl." In stereo. The women smiled at each other. "Spiral bound," Lilly added, sipping her coffee.

"It had lyrics to Cyndi Lauper's 'Girls Just Wanna Have Fun' on the cover," Esme added.

Lilly choked her coffee down and laughed through the resulting cough. "Oh my God, I hated that cover. It was so . . . *Tiger Beat.*"

All three laughed, but Danny sobered quickly.

"So what's with these cryptic questions?" Esme asked.

This was it. Now or never. "I need to read it."

Lilly balked. "You can't, Danny V. That's an invasion of privacy. And you're a *cop!*" Lilly clicked her tongue. "What would your mother say?"

"She'd say, Get your wife back, son. Whatever it takes. Besides, it isn't illegal."

Lilly sat straighter. "Yeah, but morally—"

"Hang on." Danny held up his hands. "Just listen. I don't make a habit of reading Pilar's journals"— he felt a small stab of guilt at the not-quite-true statement—"but I'm desperate. My marriage is in trouble. I won't sit idly by and watch it end." He splayed his palms on his chest. "I'll take full responsibility—"

"What's the journal's connection with your marital problems, anyway?" Esme looked intrigued.

Their wary expressions told Dan he hadn't fully explained his intention yet. He didn't even know if he could. He covered Esme's left hand, Lilly's right, with his own. "Look, I wouldn't even consider reading it if I thought there was any other way."

"To what?" Lilly shot him a narrowed scowl.

"To win her back." His estranged wife's two best friends stared at him as though he'd asked them to run a hit.

"Huh?" Lilly looked baffled and dubious all at once. "With a sixteen-year-old journal? Oooo-kayyy."

"What exactly do you intend to do?" Esme asked.

Danny grabbed his coffee cup, turning it around and around between his fingers. "See, I don't want her to take me back because she feels obligated or just gives in. I need to show her she can trust me. That I'm worthy of her love."

Lilly leaned in and snapped her fingers twice. "Danny, speak female. You aren't making a bit of sense."

"Okay, give me a chance. Man, you two are a rough audience." He cleared his throat. "I'm hoping her journal will tell me what I did right the first time." He pressed his lips together. "It's a long shot, I know. But I'm going to win her back by . . . doing whatever I did to make her fall in love with me in high school. Again."

There, he'd said it. The room hung in suspended animation. Both women stared, openmouthed. Then, as though a magic romance fairy had sprinkled

her beguiling dust over them, their surprised expressions softened into something downright
dreamy. "Awwwwww," they sighed, before exchang-
ing a chick look that made him nervous.

"Danny V, you big romantic fool." Lilly sighed.
She punched him in the arm, but her face showed
approval. "You're going to recreate your courtship?"

He hadn't imagined he could sum up his plan in
so few words, but there it was. "In a nutshell, yes."

Lilly clicked her tongue. "You really do love her,
in your own infuriating male way, don't you? That's
so sweet."

"I love her more than life itself."

"Okay, read the journal." Esme's expression was
warm. "But if Pilar finds out and flips, you're on
your own."

"Absolutely." He hung his head. When he'd recovered from the acute flush of relief, he looked up.
"Thanks for understanding."

Esme patted his hand, and Lilly said, "You never
quite know what you have until you lose it, huh,
Danny?"

"Not true. I always knew." He quirked his mouth to
the side. "I guess I just didn't know how to show it."

Nine

From Pilar Perea's neon-swirl, Cyndi Lauper journal, end of September, eleventh grade:

Oh my God, I think Danny Valenzuela is going to ask me to homecoming!!!!! I totally didn't know if we'd get back together this year after the split. Man! I get pissed every time I think about Daddy making me and Danny break up for the summer because he thought we were "getting too serious." Jump back—we haven't even been to third base! It sucked totally!!

I heard Danny went out with Renee Montoya over the summer, and I was depressed to the max. I played my soundtrack from Endless Love *over and over, crying and missing him. I hate thinking there was any other girl, but I'd rather it be anybody other than skanky Renee. If her bangs get any taller, her head will need its own zip code. Gag me with a spoon!!!*

Anyway, Danny's, like, the baddest guy in the whole school, and I want to go to homecoming with him! No—I want to marry him!! Wouldn't we have the cutest little daughters?

Pilar Valenzuela.

Mrs. Danny Valenzuela.

Pilar + Danny = 4ever

I've been stressed since school started that he found someone new. Lil says I shouldn't worry. I'd die if he took someone else, though. Noelle Ruiz (witch) said she'd heard Danny was asking Renee (skank). So, I'm not for sure he's gonna ask me. But Kathy Pirelli overheard Jay Gaston talking to Danny's friend, Ray What's-his-face—that jock—and Kathy said Jay told her he heard something like Danny was going to have Ray ask me tomorrow at lunch. Totally rad!

Anyway, I think he'll ask. He sent me a carnation on sweetheart's day. The frosh delivered them during third hour, which was bitchin' since Noelle (witch) is in my class. She was, like, totally ragged off about it. She kept staring hard at me through those spidery-stiff eyelashes. I'm sorry, I don't like that chick. She's, like, the total biggest home wrecker in our class.

One other cool thing. Esme said Danny was totally scoping me out before sixth yesterday. I knew he was standing there with Ray, so I kind of played like I didn't see them so Danny wouldn't think I was a dweeb. It's so hard not knowing what he feels. I should be totally assertive and have one of my friends ask him if he wants to get back together, but it would bite if he said no, and then I'd look like a freak. I guess I'll just wait and see if Ray asks me to go to the dance with Danny. Then I'll know once and for all.

I'm in love!!!!

If Mama and Daddy don't let me go, I'll sneak out, swear to God. This is my life, and, I mean, god, I'm sixteen years old. When are they going to start treating me like an adult??? It's so tedious!

Anyway, I'm so spazzed! I'm going to starve next week so I can lose five pounds before the dance. I want a red dress, too. This month's Glamour *said guys think red is hot. Daddy will probably have a cow. Ugh!*

I have to study, but I totally hope Danny asks me!!! Getting asked to homecoming is practically like getting an engagement ring!!! I'd know for sure he liked me then. Everyone would. Totally awesome!

Danny set the journal on the center console of the patrol car and glanced around the deserted lot where he'd parked against the closed factory building. The radio had been quiet. He usually spent downtime stopping cars and contacting suspicious people, but he'd been back at work for nearly a week, and this was the first chance he had to dig into the journal. Plus, work was the only place he *knew* Pilar wouldn't bust him.

He snapped off his red shoulder lamp, dousing the interior of the cruiser in darkness, and then just sat there with his head buzzing. Teens were so . . . *weird*. Of course, he liked knowing Pilar had considered him the "baddest guy in the whole school." A cocky grin lit his face. She'd loved him even back then. What a feeling.

But her teenage angst was exhausting to read. Amusing, too. He didn't remember them being quite so . . . well, *teenaged*. Pilar dotted every 'i' and 'j' with a little heart. Nobody escaped that gawky stage, he supposed. Odd how the years, a mortgage, and a few kids could alter a person's perspective.

He could, however, relate to Pilar's constant "he loves me, he loves me not" agony over their budding relationship. He'd felt just as needy and unsure about her, especially during that interminable summer apart before junior year. His gut clenched with the awful memory. At age seventeen, panting with puppy love, three months without Pilar Perea had been his private version of hell. But their love had endured then, and it would again.

Dan fingered the neon cover, shaking his head. Had Pilar really thought he'd have chosen another girl over her? And Renee, of all people? Everyone knew she was a skank. He barked a laugh, then a tired groan escaped. He was seriously losing his luggage on this trip down memory lane.

The truth was, he'd spent that whole miserable summer hanging with his buddies, trying not to look like the lovesick pup he was. But now he understood Mr. Perea's concern. The man had probably taken one look at Danny's face and feared for his daughter's virtue. Rightly so. At seventeen, it'd been physiologically impossible to keep his brain out of his pants. He'd wanted Mr. Perea's little girl something bad.

Still did . . .

Dan shook the enticing thoughts from his brain. Enough reminiscing. What had he learned from the journal that would help him win his wife back? First, young Pilar had yearned for confirmation that she was *his girl*. That need probably hadn't changed much. Also, she used to think an invitation to homecoming was akin to an engagement—

Whoa. He went completely still. Brainstorm.

Big brainstorm.

He checked his Ironman watch and drummed his

fingers on the steering wheel, a wholeheartedly cheesy plot formulating in his head. Oh, yeah. This idea was made-for-TV corny, but it had an odd charm. Did he dare? His embarrassed laughter rang loudly in the patrol car.

If the dreamy expressions on Esme and Lilly's faces at the coffee shop had been any indication, a woman might be able to appreciate this purely for its sappy intent. It could work if he didn't take it too seriously, and really, how could he? Plus, Pilar was worth every ounce of potential humiliation he'd feel if this didn't work.

But it would. It could.

It just so happened that his old pal Ray Falcon was the high school football coach now, and coincidentally, homecoming was two weekends away. Divine providence . . .

Snatching up his cell phone, he dialed information for Ray's number. He'd bet, for the promise of a hosted and catered pay-per-view fight night, he could bribe Ray into asking Pilar if she'd go out with "the baddest guy in the school" again. Just for old time's sake. Ray'd always been a good sport, the first to jump all over a dare. What the hell? He had everything to gain—Pilar and his life—and nothing to lose except his dignity.

Definitely dice he was willing to roll.

Almost two weeks back at work, and Danny was living up to his promises. Pilar had to give him that. He'd taken an afternoon of sick time to accompany

her and Teddy to the doctor. He got the boys
dressed and fed on the mornings she had yoga class.
He asked about her day, brought tea to her room
every night, chose home life instead of overtime.
He'd even helped her pick out college classes.

She could slowly, surely, feel trust for him seeping
back into her soul. If she weren't ten times bitten, a
hundred times shy, she might have to admit that,
yes, the wake-up call she'd given Danny had actually
worked.

Even though he'd been acting so . . . odd lately.

Not only had Danny suddenly begun playing al-
bums from their high school years, but there were
the flowers. On Monday, the daisy was on her nightstand with a note from Danny telling her how much
he loved her. Tuesday, blue bachelor's buttons had
been in the bathroom sink. The attached note spoke
of trust and commitment and second chances.
Wednesday's green carnation and Thursday's yellow
tulip? The shower and the kitchen counter, respec-
tively. One note about Pep, the second about Teddy.
Today's blood-red rose had rested atop the pillow on
Danny's side of the bed, and the note . . .

Phew, that note.

Her face flamed. She kept that particular missive
aside for her own private pleasure.

Yeah, something was definitely up with Danny.

Pilar was discussing just that with Lilly and Esme
that Friday morning when they'd gotten together to
browse the bridesmaid dress catalogs Lilly had
checked out from the wedding planner's office. The
three friends stood by the dinette and stared at the

vase of flowers. Pilar had arranged them on the table with the closed notes for her friends' examination. Danny'd even folded the letters in that silly, tucked corner way they used back in junior high.

"See?" Her sweeping gesture took in the whole display. "Isn't it freaky?"

Lilly picked up a neatly folded note and turned it over in her hand. "You used to live to get these from Danny."

"A zillion years ago, when we were young and stupid."

"So? Don't be so stuffy and adult. It's sweet," Esme said. "You don't have to be a teenager to appreciate sweet."

Pilar quirked her mouth. They weren't getting her point. Maybe this would help. She planted her hands on her hips. "You know what was playing on the stereo when I woke up today? 'Stairway to freakin' Heaven'."

"Oh, isn't that the first slow song you and Danny danced to? That's perfect!" Esme exclaimed, clapping.

"Good song, but it got really fast at the end, remember?" Lilly crinkled her nose. "You never knew whether to dance all jerky and fast or just say thanks and split. Not the easiest slow dance song, if I remember correctly."

Pilar couldn't help but chuckle. Okay, so the nostalgic music was rather charming. But strange, too. "Listen to me, you guys, I'm serious. The day before, I ate breakfast to strains of 'Always and Forever', and last Monday before bed, the man actually played Rick James's 'Super Freak'."

Lilly muffled a laugh against the side of her fist.

"Pilar, it's cute," Esme assured her. "Why are you so worried?"

She treated them to a good-natured pout. "I'm beginning to think *he* smacked his head instead of Teddy."

Lilly and Esme exchanged a smile.

"If you want my opinion, I think it's romantic and you're overreacting," Lilly said.

"I agree." Esme grinned.

"Traitors." Pilar pulled a face. "You're no help."

Lilly patted her hand. "What's wrong with a little romance, Pea?"

"Nothing. I don't know." She crossed her arms. "I suspect he's trying to butter me up."

Lilly rolled her hand. "And the problem with that is . . .?"

"I don't—" She sighed. "If you must know, it's kind of working."

"A-ha!" Esme smirked. "Just enjoy the attention, Pilar. Romantic gestures aren't meant to be analyzed to death."

Lilly flicked her hand over and studied her nails with nonchalance. "How's it going since Danny went back to work?"

Pilar's stomach swirled with an unfamiliar feeling of hope and anticipation. "Great so far. It's been exactly how I always knew it could be. But . . . it's lulling me into a feeling of false security." Heat prickled over her skin, followed closely by chagrin. "I'm starting to forget how bad things had gotten and focus on whether or not it would be wise to jump his bones."

"Do it!" Esme urged.

Pilar bit her lip. She wanted to. So much. If only Danny had acted this wonderful from the get-go. "What if it's the calm before the storm?"

Lilly rolled her eyes. "Damn, Pea. Have you ever stopped to consider that maybe the storm already ripped up your coast and moved on? This might just be the cleanup part, you know, like after a hurricane." She reached out to touch the red rose. "Think of these flowers as Red Cross volunteers who've come to patch things up and rebuild docks."

Pilar and Esme started laughing. "Oh my God, Lil is waxing poetic. We need to marry her off, and soon." Pilar snapped her fingers softly and held out her hand. "Enough. Give me those dress catalogs. We have to make sure you don't costume us like bright little crumpets for the wedding."

"Oh, but check this out." Lilly opened a catalog to the picture of a very brief, very tight fuschia gown with holes running up both sides. She sucked in her cheeks. "Better crumpets than strumpets."

The old friends erupted into laughter again, just as the doorbell chimed. Still chuckling, Pilar headed toward the door. She opened it, expecting a neighbor or FedEx—anyone but a man she couldn't place but vaguely recognized. He stood there looking uncomfortable. Though he wore a baseball cap, gray showed at his temples, and he had the deeply weathered face of one who'd spent his life outdoors. Their high school mascot was embroidered on the jacket of his nylon jogging suit. She smiled. "Yes?"

He grinned, looking younger than she had initially pegged him. "Wow, Pilar Perea, you haven't changed a bit unless you count being more gorgeous than ever."

That voice! Her jaw dropped. No way! It was Danny's old high school buddy in disguise as an actual grown-up. Ray . . . Ray . . . What's-his-face. That's it!

"Ray!" She pushed the storm door open and stood aside. "Come in. I haven't seen you in, gosh, years!"

He removed the hat and smoothed his fingers through his hair jock-style—once, twice, three times, front to back. "It has been a while, that's for sure."

She gave him a quick hug, then pulled away, curious about his sudden reappearance in her life. Just seeing him made her want to don leg warmers and rip a sweatshirt so it hung off one shoulder. She felt like she'd stumbled back in time.

I'm a maaaaaniac, maaaaaniac . . .

"Danny's running errands. You remember Lilly Lujan and Esme Jaramillo, right?" She turned toward the breakfast nook without waiting for an answer. "Hey, you guys, come here."

They bustled through the archway, and Pilar couldn't help but notice that her friends didn't look nearly as suprised as she felt to see a lifesize high school flashback standing in the living room like it was *normal.*

Lilly strode forward. "Well, whaddya know, it's Ray What's-his-face." She shook his hand. "Good to see you."

Ray chuckled, slanting Pilar a glance. "I forgot Pilar used to call me that. Ray *Falcon.*" He nodded to Lilly. "So, the most famous person from our graduating class. My wife has your *Cosmo* cover tucked in our yearbook."

"Hey, I have it in mine, too." Lilly deftly deflected the compliment with a casual toss of her hair. "I might be the most recognizable, but Esme's making a much bigger contribution to the world. She's a research scientist."

"That I know. Hey, Es." He offered a firm handshake. "In addition to coaching at the high school, I teach AP science. Dr. Jaramillo-Mendez speaks to my genetics students once a year." He winked and nodded to her belly. "I guess you're expecting a little clone of your own, huh?"

Esme beamed, her fists bracing her lower back. "And not a moment too soon."

"I hear you." He tugged the wallet from his back pocket and opened it to expose an accordian of photos featuring smiling brown children. "We've got seven. Round about the seventh month of each pregnancy, I always started to fear for my life."

"Seven!" Esme looked vaguely ill. "You are speaking to a very pregnant woman, need I remind you. You should fear for your life right this minute."

Ray feigned a terrified duck when Esme raised her fists, then provided names as Lilly pawed through his proud papa snapshots.

Weirder by the minute. Pilar cleared her throat. "A father of seven is the perfect candidate for coffee." She inclined her head toward the kitchen. "Would you care to join us for a cup? Danny should be home shortly."

"Ah, no. Thanks, but I'm due back at the school

soon. It's my planning period." He tugged his collar, mottled redness climbing his neck. "I actually came to talk to you."

"Me?" Pilar tilted her face to the side. "What's up?"

He cleared his throat, shooting an almost apologetic glance over her shoulder toward Esme and Lilly. "Yeah, uh. Well, I was just, uh, wondering . . ." He chuckled, then shrugged, the grin tooling deep lines into his handsome, leathery cheeks. "Danny wanted me to ask you if you might be interested in going to homecoming with him."

Ahhhh . . . huh? The entire room and everything in it froze. No one moved. No one spoke. No one drew a breath. Pilar felt like Samantha on *Bewitched* just after she did that nose thing, but Pilar knew, in her case, the magic couldn't last. She had to speak, to respond somehow.

Danny sent a pal to ask her out?

Finally she managed a half choke, half laugh, splaying a hand she couldn't feel on a chest that would surely explode if it expanded another millimeter. "You . . . you're kidding, right?"

Ray clapped the baseball cap back on his head, settling it just so. "Nope. The dance is in two weeks, after the game, and this is your invite. Just like old times, eh?"

She held up a finger, blinking rapidly and moving her mouth like a fish. "Let me get this straight. Homecoming."

"Yup."

"In two weeks."

"Bingo."

"And my husband of fourteen years enlisted your help in asking me out? For a date? To homecoming?"

He winked. "Some things don't change."

"Oh, Pea," Lilly jostled Pilar's shoulders. "It's the most romantic thing I've ever heard."

Pilar darted a dazed glance at Esme, the more sensible friend. But, no. Es had her hands clasped at her chest and tears shining in her eyes. Pilar wanted to write it off to pregnancy hormones, but . . . she couldn't.

"So?" Ray smoothed his palms together slowly. "Can I tell Danny yes, or do you already have another date?"

Her breath left her in a whoosh, and she sagged. This was absurd. Unheard of. This was . . . this was . . . one of the sweetest things Danny Valenzuela had ever done. Her heart melted. "Of course I don't have another date, Ray What's-his-face Falcon. I'm thirty-two years old, for God's sake."

"So that's a yes?"

Pilar threaded her fingers into her hair and stared at him. This was so unexpected, she didn't have the proper words. After a moment, she made some ineffective nodlike motions with her head. "Hell, why not?" She laughed, feeling light and silly. "Tell him I'd love to."

Lilly and Esme cheered.

Even Ray looked triumphant. "Great." He turned to leave, then snapped his fingers and spun back. "Almost forgot. Dan will pick you up at seven for dinner."

"Pick me up?" She frowned. "But he lives here."

"Not that night. He wants it to be perfect."

Excitement tingled her flesh. "Okay."

Ray touched the bill of his cap and nodded to Lilly and Esme before glancing back at Pilar. "One other thing. Dan suggested you wear something red." He looked smug. "Guys think red is hot. Did you know that?"

Ten

From Pilar Valenzuela's journal, homecoming night:

I haven't felt this excited about seeing Danny in a long time. He dropped the boys at Esme and Gavino's house yesterday to spend the weekend and packed a bag for himself—to stay with Ruben, I assume. In any case, he hasn't been around. This morning, however, I awoke to find a gift certificate for a spa day at a local salon tucked beneath a hot cappuccino. Sneaky.

Every time I think about it, my stomach swirls. It's truly like falling in love all over again.

So now I've been massaged, salted, mud-packed, manicured, pedicured, waxed, and coiffed, and I feel like a queen awaiting the arrival of her royal court. Except in the most rudimentary way, Danny and I haven't discussed tonight too much. It's been almost as if neither of us wanted to break the spell. And what a spell it is. The touch of mystery has only added to my anticipation. That and the fact that my new red dress fits like a dream and makes me feel utterly sexy. God bless stress for its slimming side effects. (Yoga and walking helped, too.)

I feel like we're on a threshold of a new beginning.

Danny and I have weathered the storm. We still have work to do, but I feel like we can . . . finally. I'm ready to put the past behind us and move on with our marriage.

Me<---hopeful. And in love.

I can't wait for him to arrive and take me to homecoming. But only because that's one step closer to when he can take me home. . . .

The doorbell rang, and Pilar's pulse kicked into overdrive. Oh, God. The moment of truth. Smoothing her moist palms against the ruby-red crushed velvet covering her curves, she headed to the door and pulled it open.

Danny.

In a coal-black, athletic cut suit over a light gray silk shirt, he looked edible, and she was starving. The open neck of his shirt offered an inviting peek at his chest—a good place to start the feast. A perfect red rosebud adorned his lapel, and the room felt suddenly more alive for his presence.

His expression flashed with surprise and awe, then deepened into something feral as his eyes traveled her body like a Porsche hugged the open road. "Lord almighty, Pilar. If you've ever looked hotter, I can't remember."

Her tummy flopped, and she actually had the urge to titter. Instead she backed up and spun for him, treating him to a full view of the dress she'd found only after trying about fifty others. All red. Did he have any idea how hard it was to find fifty red dresses in one city? "You like?"

"I love. Can I come in?"

She swept her arm aside. "It's your house."

"Yeah?" His eyes looked wistful as he reached out and trailed one finger just inside the edge of her neckline.

She bit her lip, suddenly scared.

As though sensing her fear, Danny crossed the threshold, but stood away. A mischievous smile spread across his face, and Pilar noticed he had one hand behind his back.

Lighter tone. Good choice. She cleared her throat and lifted her chin toward the hand she couldn't see. "Whatcha got back there?"

"Something for you." He rocked from heel to toe playfully.

"Hmm. A corsage?"

He frowned. "Damn, I knew I forgot something."

"That's okay." She tossed her trimmed and styled hair. "I wouldn't want to pin it on this dress anyway."

"Mmmmm, yes. That dress," he drawled, his gaze as disreputable as his tone.

She crossed her arms and watched him look hungrily at her cleavage. Sometimes being a woman wanted by a man felt more powerful than sorcery. "If not a corsage, then . . . wine?"

His grin was wolfish and enticingly uncouth. "You think you'd be safe around me with wine on the menu? In that"—he swallowed tightly—"dress?"

Not in it for long. Her chin lifted primly, but she bit her bottom lip. "Is it candy?"

"Silly to give candy to a woman as sweet as you." He shook his head. "Three strikes. You're out."

Laughing, she reached out. "Okay, mister. Give it up."

And suddenly she held a plush white teddy bear wearing a miniature letter jacket. "Oh, Danny!"

He looked pleased with himself. "I would've worn mine, but it was too tight through the shoulders."

Pilar clutched the bear with both hands, grinning down into his black button eyes. "This looks exactly like the bear I wanted—"

"In eleventh grade, for Valentine's day."

Her head shot up and her brows dipped. "How'd you remember?" Come to think of it, he'd been remembering a whole lot about high school lately. She began to ponder this. "Tell me how you remembered."

He feigned indignance, deftly sidestepping a straight answer. "Are you saying I have a poor memory?"

"You really wanna go there, D?" Her expression epitomized drollness.

Again, he turned serious and almost predatory. He reached out and cupped her waist, pulling her against him. His eyes traced the lines of her face, her chest, her mouth. "Uh-uh. That's not where I want to go. Actually, I don't want to *go* anywhere. What I want to do is come home. *Really* come home."

Her breath caught, and she knew nothing beyond the aching throb that had begun at her core and the blinding need to feel his mouth on hers. This, *this* was how things had felt between Danny Valenzuela and Pilar Perea. This fire was what had burned them to trembling ashes the first six years of their marriage. What she'd missed so desperately, what she wanted worse than air for her next breath. "I want that, too."

"You see this look on my face, Punkybean?" he whispered, low and sexy-rough. "This expression that says I want to be inside you? Now. Here. You see that?"

"Yes," she sighed.

"That's what your Daddy saw that made him split us up that summer." He bent forward and nipped her ear, pulling her black pearl earring into his mouth. Hot against her cheek, he rumbled, "I wanted Daddy's baby girl. Wanted to see how fast I could get past her innocence and make her mine. Forever."

She clutched his sleeve, leaning her head back to expose the rough pulse in her throat to his famished, urgent kisses. "Danny."

A low, animal sound came from his throat as he pulled aside the neckline of her dress and sucked on her exposed shoulder, warm and hot and wet.

Her body sagged against his, and the teddy bear fell to the floor. His hands smoothed over her back to her buttocks, cupping, claiming. "Keep this up and we'll never make it to the dance."

"Oh"—he licked her collarbone—"we're gonna make it to the dance." He hovered over her and kissed the tops of her breasts exposed by the dress's plunging neckline. "I'm just giving you something to think about"—his tongue traced her lips—"while we're stuck in that darkened gymnasium."

He took her in a breath-stopping kiss, backing her slowly until she was pressed against the wall, but pulled away at the sound of her throaty laugh. "You laughed at me the first time I kissed you, too. What now?"

She shook her head. "You are an evil, horrid tease."

"Oh, no way. I'm not teasing at all, baby girl." As if to prove it, he ground against her. Once, then again. "We're only going to the dance so I can bring you home from it."

"Just like high school," she groused lightly.

"Just like always, Punky. I want you something bad. I'm never gonna let you doubt that again."

Feeling weak and wet and shaky, she pushed him away. He might think they were headed to the dance, but if he kept talking in that stonewashed velvet tone, the only dancing they'd be doing was between the sheets. "Well, then, let me go fix my ruined lipstick, and we can leave."

She swiveled on her high black heels and sauntered toward the hall, making sure he saw every slow-motion sway.

"Whoooey. I need a swing like that in my backyard."

Pilar laughed over her shoulder. "You used to say that to me in high school!" He looked smug, and not at all surprised, she noticed. Had they slipped into a time machine? If so, lock the door. She'd stay right here in the flames with Danny, sizzling away.

The brash bathroom light slapped her with the present, illuminating her true colors. Swollen lips, drowsy eyes. She clapped her cheeks. Oh, God. She wanted him. Bad. Why couldn't she have a poker face when it came to him? As she lined her lips and filled in the crimson color, she heard Danny swear viciously from the living room. Warning tightened her gut, and she peered around the corner, down the hall. "What's wrong?"

He didn't answer. She shrugged. Her imagination.

She blotted her lipstick on a tissue, fluffed her hair, and headed down the hall. "What are you swearing about?" Her eyes dropped to his hands . . . hands holding his work pager. She felt her world start to shred, her defenses drop into place. *Don't say it!* "Danny. What is it?"

Troubled brown eyes raised to hers. "I got paged."

Her chest began to tremble. She crossed her arms, already feeling him slipping away. "Don't **call** back."

He flipped one hand over. "It's the emergency page, Pilar. I should—" he cut himself off, pressing his lips in a thin line. *"Damn it.* Why this now?"

All Pilar could see, all she could feel was her precious dream crashing down around her. The pain ripped through her, worse this time. She knew she wouldn't survive it. "Are you going to call?"

He remained silent, head hung, the muscle in his jaw ticking.

"Danny?"

Their eyes locked, gazes filled with pleading and pain. Desperation. Indesision.

Self-preservation flared, and Pilar threw her arms up. "Call work. Just go ahead. I never have been able to stop you." She stormed down the hall away from him and slammed into their bedroom. Her hands shook with adrenaline and disappointment. She kicked out of her heels and paced the dark room from end to end, raging at the unfairness of it all.

Yanking off her earrings, she tossed them on the dresser, gulping back a sob.

No. No crying.

She leaned her back against the door and closed her eyes. She was so stupid. *So* stupid. She should've seen this coming a mile off. Nothing had changed, nothing ever wou—

"Nora, hi. It's Dan," Pilar heard him say. "Listen . . . I can't come in. Whatever it is will have to—"

He went dead silent, and Pilar couldn't help but crack the door and listen. Had he really said he couldn't come in?

"Jesus, no. How the hell did that happen? Where?"

His voice had gone hoarse and shaky. Acid lurched in Pilar's gut. She knew that tone. She opened the door and stood in the hallway, staring down at Danny whose back was to her. His shoulders slumped with defeat.

"Oh, God. Not O'Doyle. His wife is just about ready to deliver twins." Danny bit out a rough curse and swirled his palm over his head. "Where'd he take the bullets?"

Pilar's stomach plunged and stars rushed her eyes. A cop had been hurt. A cop she knew, who worked Danny's shift. *It could've been him.* As the room dimmed to a sickening black pinpoint, she grappled for the wall to steady herself.

His next words were strained, halting. Underlying his words, she heard shame, futility. "Nora . . . you know what's been going on with me. If you can . . . get anyone else to cover—"

"Wait!" This was wrong. He shouldn't sound like that.

He spun to face her, hope and fear in his eyes.

With the sudden clarity of a roundhouse kick to the chest, Pilar realized how grossly unfair she was being to Danny. He'd done so much changing, made so many compromises. What had she done to make things better between them? Jack, that's what. If she wanted him to consider her feelings and needs, she needed to reciprocate. And if Danny had been the cop who'd taken the bullets, she'd damn well want every single one of his coworkers to drop their lives to help him out. No questions asked. Shame threatened to choke her as she drooped under the realization and remorse about her selfishness.

"Hang on." Danny cupped the receiver. "Pilar?"

"O'Doyle got shot?"

"Yeah. And a couple of bystanders."

She squeezed her eyes shut, gulping back nausea. "You have to go."

"No, P. Not if it means—"

"It doesn't." She closed the distance between them, pressing her palm against his cheek. "I . . . I have no right. You have to go, Danny. I know that. I was . . . selfish."

His chest rose and fell a couple times, then he lifted the receiver. "Let me call you back in two minutes." A pause. "Yeah." He cut the connection.

"I'm sorry," she whispered.

"I won't go if it means losing you. I'm serious."

"Danny, I've been unfair." She chewed her lip. "You have a life, other than us—"

"No." His head shook vehemently. "You are my life."

"I know. Honey, I know." Her heart nearly breaking, she smiled and shook her head. "I meant that you have other responsibilities."

His Adam's apple rose and fell, then he nodded slowly.

"Go take care of them." On tiptoe, she rained kisses on his lips. "I want you to."

He pulled her against his chest and deepened the kiss, driving his fingers up into the back of her hair. He took her like a starving man, breaths ragged and fast. Finally he pulled away, both of them gasping for air. "We'll miss homecoming."

"No, we won't." She rubbed her thumb over the nearly invisible scar on his chin. "You go be a cop, and we'll have homecoming right here when you're done."

He stilled, cradling her face between his hands, his eyes searching hers. "You're sure?"

"I've never been more sure, Danny Valenzuela. I love you, and . . . nothing's gonna change that. I'll be right here waiting."

The house looked dark and still when Dan headed up the walk. He couldn't hold back the pang of disappointment, but it *was* late. Thank God, it looked like O'Doyle would recover in time to welcome his baby twins into the world. He'd been lucky, considering the bullet had entered his chest through the unprotected armhole of his Kevlar vest.

The case was huge, as one of the bystanders had

died from his injuries. Dan couldn't help but feel grateful he was alive and coming home to his family.

He worked the key carefully in case Pilar had drifted off. No sense waking her. He felt certain they had all the time in the world to celebrate like he'd planned to tonight. Another night would have to do. Still . . . disappointing. He pushed the door open slowly, but to his surprise, the house wasn't dark. It was candlelit. His eyes danced over the glow-softened interior before settling on the hand-lettered sign on the wall:

DANNY VALENZUELA'S HOMECOMING
FOLLOW THE CHOCOLATES

A smile teased its way onto his face and his heart began to pound with anticipation as he located the first Hershey's kiss on the floor. He stooped to pick it up, then noticed a second, and a third—a whole silver trail of them leading through the living room, into the breakfast nook—

He stopped short. Uh-oh. Clearly busted.

A circle of votive candles glowed and flickered on the table, and in the middle of them sat a red-leather journal. A note on the front read, *You've read the rest, now read the best.* Dan shook his head and laughed softly. He'd been so careful with that damned Cyndi Lauper journal. How could he have tripped himself up?

He popped a chocolate into his mouth and reached for the journal. The cover felt rich and smooth, and the color reminded him of that shimmery soft dress Pilar had been wearing earlier. The dress that had just begged to be ripped off. His body tightened. He suppressed a shiver of raw need, opened the book, and began reading:

If you're reading this, then you've probably figured out that I know you read my journal. Thought you could slip one over on your wife, huh? Ha ha ha, silly man. You must admit how unusual it looked when you suddenly started "remembering" stuff from the past. Memory has never been your strong point, you know. I put two and two together, then threatened Esme and Lilly with their lives if they didn't confirm my suspicions. Don't you know women hold stuff over on each other for leverage in just such situations?

But don't worry. I'm not mad.

Me<---totally reasonable woman.

Oh, Danny, you know I didn't write those journals to keep anything from you. My journal was the one place I could always express my feelings without my mother telling me "good girls grin and bear it." I love her, I just don't want to live her life. In writing, my true feelings always came out, as I'm sure you read. I only wish I would've realized I could express those emotions with you. Consider this the first entry in our journal. It turns me on thinking I can write whatever I want in here to you. You can do the same. No secrets. I can't tell you how romantic it is that you'd go to so much trouble to win me back, Danny.

Pat yourself on the back—it worked like a charm.

I've had a lot of time to think this evening, and I want you to know a few things. First, I love you. I want you back as my husband, forever. I have never wanted anyone but you, and I'm sorry we've gone through so much lately.

But we survived, yeah?

Somehow deep inside me, I always knew we would.

I hate to think what might've happened if you hadn't been so persistent.

I'm going to make you a couple of promises. I promise to be more open with you. I won't hold things in like I've always done. I promise I will never, ever make you choose between my love and your responsibilities again. That was unfair, and I feel horrible about it. Keeping this marriage together isn't solely your responsibility. Know that. I'll work on myself, too, I promise.

I promise things won't ever get so silent in this house again, and I promise the past is the past. Ah, yes. You better also believe that I promise we'll never go six months without making love again.

On that note, I have a few promises I'd like you to make. Promise you'll always need me. And want me. Promise you'll always look at me in the way that'll make my daddy go for the shotgun. Promise we'll be together forever, Danny Valenzuela, and that nothing will ever come between us again. Oh yes, promise you'll never play Rick James's "Super Freak" to warm me up. (ha ha)

And, Danny? Promise me you'll think about us trying for a baby girl. I've always thought we'd make such adorable daughters. I'm ready whenever you are.

One last request . . . promise you'll grab the champagne from the fridge before you come into our bedroom. I told you I'd be waiting for you when you got home.

Well . . . you're home, D. And, I'm waiting.

Emotion slammed Dan in the chest. The words on these pages were written in the hand of a woman, not a girl anymore. He loved both versions of Pilar, but this woman was his wife, and she always would be. She loved him enough to give him another chance. His nostrils flared and his throat ached with pure, unadulterated love, as the words blurred before his eyes.

Dan set the journal aside and crossed to the fridge. A cold bottle of Mumm champagne and a bowl of ripe strawberries occupied the bottom shelf. With a surge of desire, he retrieved them.

Knowing it would be a long, sweet ride, and not wanting one moment of it interrupted by the fire department kicking down his door, he took a moment to blow out all the candles on the table and in the living room. The delay was agonizing, but sometimes a sharp jab of pain was just the thing to bring a man back to life.

He crept down the hallway and eased open the door to find the bedroom blazing with candlelight, too. The air smelled of wax and woman. His wife. The golden glow gilded Pilar's bare skin . . . skin barely covered by the red silk teddy and thigh-high hose. He wanted to fall on the ground and weep with gratitude for being privy to such beauty. Instead, he moved to the edge of the bed and sat down. For a minute they just stared at each other, warmth and love and forgiveness stretching between them, binding them in commitment forever.

Dan reached out and toyed with her wedding ring. "I promise," he whispered.

Her chin quivered. She reached for him. "Me too."

With a groan of submission and possession, a love so strong it blocked out everything but this moment, he swept her into his arms and captured her mouth with his own. She tasted both sweet and sultry, felt both familiar and completely new. Pilar. His soul mate. Thank God for second chances.

Pulling away, he lost himself in her big brown eyes, swallowing back the knot in his throat. That familiar sweet ache filled him, and he said the only words that came to mind, the only appropriate statement for this moment.

"I love you, Pilar Valenzuela. Forever—"

"And a day?"

With a chuckle, he shook his head, then slowly kissed his way down her body. "Not long enough, baby girl. Not nearly long enough."

COMING IN APRIL 2001
FROM ENCANTO ROMANCE

__WILD FOR YOU
by Victoria Marquez   0-7860-1219-6 $3.99US/4.99CAN
Clay Blackthorne pledges to protect Marisol Calderon upon her brother's request. So he takes a job as a security specialist in Marisol's apartment building where he can protect her from the person who is stalking her. When the threatening advances of this stranger ensue, Clay proposes that they marry to thwart her stalker. What begins as a charade will soon end in love.

__ONLY A KISS AWAY
by Lourdes Carvajal   0-7860-1244-7 $3.99US/$4.99CAN
Mercedes Garcia is recovering after a bitter divorce, so the last thing she is looking for is a blind date. But her best friend needs to find someone to escort her Costa Rican brother to a dance. Confident that he will return to Costa Rica, Mercedes sees no harm in spending time with him. But when Joquin finally returns to Costa Rica and cannot forget the love that he found, he returns to America—and Mercedes—for good.
